The Hiring Fair

by

Laura Strickland

Help Wanted Series

This is a work of fiction. Names, characters, places, and incidents are either the product of the author's imagination or are used fictitiously, and any resemblance to actual persons living or dead, business establishments, events, or locales, is entirely coincidental.

The Hiring Fair

COPYRIGHT © 2016 by Laura Strickland

Cover Art by *Diana Carlile*

The Wild Rose Press, Inc.
PO Box 708
Adams Basin, NY 14410-0708
Visit us at www.thewildrosepress.com

Publishing History
First Tea Rose Edition, 2016
Print ISBN 978-1-5092-0812-8
Digital ISBN 978-1-5092-0813-5

Help Wanted Series
Published in the United States of America

"Before we go inside, I want to be sure I ha' your understanding. This is no' an ordinary marriage but something more in the manner of a hiring, which is why I came to the fair in the first place."

He inclined his shaggy head toward her slightly. "A hiring wi'out wages. That is against the law, you do ken."

She swept him with her gaze. "And are you a man to adhere to arbitrary laws? I confess, I did no' get that impression."

"And," he returned, "are you a woman who needs to hire a husband?" He echoed her. "I confess, I did no' get *that* impression." He returned her stare, slow and attentive. "You are certainly bonnie enough to snare a husband the usual way."

To her surprise, Annie felt a wave of heat course through her. "I do no' want a usual kind o' husband. I want one who will tak' my orders and stay clear o' my bed. Be sure you are that man before we go inside and speak these vows."

One of Sutherland's eyebrows quirked up. "I was right at the outset; you are mad."

"So we ha' already determined," Annie agreed, beginning to grow edgy again. What if he refused at this late moment? Where would she find a substitute, with the market now deserted and the snow falling? Besides, she discovered she did not want a substitute; for reasons she did not quite understand, she wanted this man and no other.

Praise for Laura Strickland

"The world building is phenomenal."

~*Daysie W. at My Book Addiction and More*
~*~

"Laura Strickland creates a world that not only draws you in, but she incorporates it…seamlessly…the kind of book that keeps you awake well into the wee hours, and sighing with satisfaction when you've finished the very last page."

~*Nicole McCaffrey, author*
~*~

"As I read I became so involved with the story, I found it difficult to put down the book.…Definitely…an author to watch."

~*Dandelion at Long & Short Reviews*

Dedication

In honor of my ancestress, Annie King,
who read the tea leaves and passed down her wisdom.

Books by Laura Strickland
available from The Wild Rose Press, Inc.

A word about hiring fairs…

Hiring fairs have been common in Britain since the 1300s. Traditionally, they were large annual gatherings where farm workers and landholders met so workers might be taken on for the season. The rate of wage was often set ahead of time and a worker would agree to stay till the next fair. These events eventually evolved to include all the trappings of such gatherings, including food, vendors, and music.

Dates of the gatherings varied by district. In England, they were held after the harvest in late October or early November. My research indicates that in Scotland, hiring fairs were often held on or around March 10th, so I have set my story accordingly.

Chapter One
Oban, Western Scotland, March 1810

Tam Sutherland had nearly given up all hope when the madwoman climbed onto the platform.

The hiring fair—largest in the district—drew much too swiftly to a close. All day he'd stood while the sun rose high overhead illuminating the market and bringing out the combined scents of sea kelp, damp earth, and too many people gathered in close proximity, until now it sank like a fiery eye toward a bank of cloud in the west. He'd watched farmer after farmer and a few agents from larger estates climb the platform where the madwoman now stood and announce what sort of workers they wished to hire. He'd seen man after man and more than a few lasses get taken on. He'd even circulated among them, inquiring from everyone whether they needed additional help, but none would consent to employ a man such as Tam.

After walking ten miles to get here, he had nothing left—no coin in his pocket, no soles on his shoes. No food had passed his lips in two days, and desperation clenched his guts as hard as the hunger. Only his dignity remained, and precious little of that.

A mere handful of potential workers remained to hear the madwoman—Tam and a few fellows bent with age, one or two scrawny striplings, and a burly fellow so drunk he could barely stand—in short, the dregs of

1

the dregs. The madwoman lifted her chin and looked past them all. He'd wondered about her earlier in the day, when he saw her moving through the crowd all on her own, sizing up prospective hirelings. A man could not easily overlook such a woman—tall, with a bold, dark eye and dressed so flamboyantly in a green hooded cape and a hat with a broad brim and a long brown feather. She wore rings on her fingers that flashed when she moved. But she did not look wealthy, for all that, and the quick, clever expression on her face betrayed her as being something beyond a common goodwife.

She'd eyed Tam right well at the outset, looked him up and down. But like everyone else she soon noticed his mangled hand and dismissed him from her consideration. Who wanted a farm worker with only one good hand? It defied reason.

Now, though, it appeared she intended to state her requirements, and Tam's heart stirred. Odd to look upon she might be, but even a place with her would be better than sleeping tonight in a ditch.

She cleared her throat and, in a voice which carried like that of a crow, called out, "I am in need of help on my holding! Gather round all of you who ha' not yet found a place."

A few people drifted up, no doubt out of curiosity. Most of them, Tam could see, were farmers with their hirelings already in tow. Folks who were prepared to leave the fair, their tasks done, paused to listen.

Tam edged closer and, out of habit, cradled his mangled hand against his chest.

Still in that clear, somehow powerful voice, the woman called, "Listen to me. 'Tis no ordinary situation, this. I am looking for a man not just for this season but many seasons. A permanent place."

Those gathered hummed and murmured over that. Such offers came but rarely; workers considered themselves fortunate to get hired on for the spring through harvest, when the work on a farm increased. Especially now when so many went about Scotland dispossessed of their own lands.

"What's the pay, mistress?" called one of the elders who, like Tam, still lacked a place.

She turned her gaze on the man, and something in her expression sent a small tremor up Tam's spine.

"No wage for this position, my good man."

"No wage!" the oldster returned, and walked off in disgust.

The crowd tittered. Many lost interest and walked away also. Curiosity and the tenuous last threads of hope kept Tam where he stood.

Would he be willing to work solely for his keep? Better, almost, to indenture himself in return for passage to the new world.

His lips twisted bitterly. And even in the new world, who would accept a man with but one good hand?

The madwoman, perhaps sensing she fast lost the attention of her listeners, stiffened. For the first time a flash of uncertainty crossed her face. Her fine, dark eyes narrowed and, proving herself mad entirely, she called, "I am no' looking for a hand, but a husband. And a woman does no' pay her husband a wage."

The crowd, like one great beast, went silent at that as if mutually taken aback. Then came the hooting and the comments, most of them bawdy, all hurled at her like stones.

"Fine work that, lady—and my back is strong enough for it!"

"Aye so, and you're saying the payment lies between your pretty thighs?"

The madwoman endured the onslaught as she might a sudden spurt of rain. Disappointment touched Tam's heart. Had he truly hoped for saving at this late hour? Aye, and she must be raving. What sort of person climbed up on the hiring platform and made such an offer?

"Nay, but," she called with no less volume, "I am in earnest."

The onlookers shook their heads, spat, and began to move away with those they'd hired—for better or worse—in train. Night now gathered in the east, and many had a long trip home. Even such a spectacle as this could not hold them long.

Only the desperate—and the intoxicated—stood on. That meant Tam, one green lad, two oldsters, and the burly drunk with the bushy black beard.

Consternation now showed clearly on the madwoman's face. She ran her gaze over the dwindling group of prospects, and Tam half expected her to jump down and fade into the growing darkness like some product of his fevered mind.

"I'll go wi' ye, mistress," the drunk called lasciviously. He returned her stare twice as boldly. "I'm liking the looks o' the provisions."

"You? You're so full of ale you can barely stand."

"Aye, but I will perform the job for ye, as you will see right well, soon as you take me to your bed."

"No." The madwoman looked about again, a bit desperately this time. Her gaze skipped over Tam, who stood front and center, ranged wide to touch the departing crowd, and returned to him. As Tam had expected, she descended from the platform, moving with sweeping dignity.

The oldster standing next to Tam, white-haired, with stringy arms and grizzled whiskers on his chin, shot him a look.

"Here she comes, lad—appears 'tis to be either you or me."

"She canno' be serious," Tam returned. "Raving, no doubt." Who in her right mind came to a hiring fair to find a husband?

"No doubt," the oldster grunted. "Still, I imagine you are more likely to get up to what she needs than I."

Tam smiled wryly. "I would ha' to be mad as her, to take such a prospect."

"Would you?" The old man nodded to the woman who now approached them. "That's a fine-looking lass."

So she was, a truth that had not escaped Tam earlier despite all her odd trappings. She seemed to flow at him like the night, the green cloak swirling about her and her eyes fixed on him like those of a cat stalking prey.

Ah, so she actually meant to speak to him, did she? He drew himself up from his sole-less shoes to his overgrown head. Shabby he might be, but he'd be damned if those last shreds of pride did not stand him in good stead.

She paused in front of Tam, and he felt rather than saw the oldster fade away. Once more she inspected him, using more care this time, her eyes as dark as the sky overhead.

"You must ha' heard my offer." Her voice had lost its crow's squawk and become soft as aged whisky.

"I did," he returned and wondered how best to deal with a madwoman. With humor, perhaps. "A fine offer of marriage." He made a show of looking around them. "Yet it appears most your prospects ha' flown."

She failed to respond to his attempted levity. "What is wrong wi' your hand?"

Aye so, direct and unsparing, was she? Tam lifted the limb in question so she might see it better in the growing dusk. "An injury. 'Twas crushed." *Stones falling, flame leaping, unbearable pain, not all of the flesh.* "Did no' heal right."

"Shame." Her deep gaze flitted over him yet again, this time in a manner surprisingly titillating. "But perhaps on my farm—"

"I'll go wi' ye, mistress." The burly fellow with the black beard came stumbling over, preceded by a wave of ale fumes strong enough to knock Tam down. "I promise I can gi' what ye need."

The madwoman's nostrils pinched with disgust. "I told you, man, you're drunk—stinking drunk."

"Nay, but that will no' last," the sot rejoined, "and a fine lass like you will sure ha' me standing for the job."

"I am no' a lass," the madwoman retorted. "Take yoursel' off."

"Nay, but gi' us a kiss and you will see right fine the stuff o' which I am made."

The madwoman took a step back, and the drunk blundered after. Tam halted the fellow's progress by planting his left hand in the center of the burly chest.

"Do as the lady says and tak' yoursel' off. Or do I

ha' to persuade you?"

The drunk grunted a breath that nearly curled Tam's hair—and fell down.

The madwoman reached out and grasped Tam's arm. A thrill went through him all the way from his fingers to his spine. What was this, then? He narrowed his gaze on her and, for a long moment during which neither of them breathed, she returned his stare.

"Well," the madwoman said then, "if it is no' a hero." She towed him away from the prone drunk, who lay groaning, and into the shadows behind the platform.

"As I was saying, the fact you ha' no' been hired may be to my good fortune. The place is yours if you want it."

"The place of—?"

"My husband."

Tam drew a deep breath. She still clutched his arm, and the ensuing waves of sensation made it hard to think. "You are serious about that, then?"

"Deadly serious. I need help at my place, and I need it at once—in the form of a husband."

"But you do know not so much as my name!"

She tipped her head. "What is your name?"

"Tam Sutherland."

She seemed to consider him again, and with more than just her eyes this time—as if her very soul searched him. "Tam, eh? Well, Tam Sutherland, if you will come wi' me now, to the priest—"

He jerked away from her. "Tonight? 'Tis no' possible."

"I assure you, it is. I ha' already made the arrangements."

"You are mad!"

She smiled a little. "Quite possibly. Nevertheless, that is the offer I am making: I ha' a small farm some five miles east of here. I can pay you no wage, but as my husband you will have your keep."

This time Tam eyed her up and down, experiencing again that small prick of arousal. As the day waned, the thought had indeed crossed his mind he would be more than happy to work for his keep and a place to lay his head. Now, though, it seemed he would have to be as mad as she, to agree.

"Why do you hesitate, Tam Sutherland? You will no' get taken on elsewhere, wi' that hand."

Frankly, he told her, "Like our intoxicated friend, I am wondering about the other duties o' a husband, lady."

For the first time she drew back from him slightly. "Och, that. Nay, that will no' be necessary."

Tam's ensuing disappointment shocked him. Aye, though—probably just as well. The last thing he needed was to climb into bed with a madwoman.

"And, lady, do you ha' a name?"

"Annie MacCallum," she replied. "So, man, what is your decision?"

Tam glanced once more around the fair. Nearly everyone had gone; even the drunk must have pulled himself up from the ground and wandered off while they spoke. Clouds gathered in the west, chased inland from the sea by a cold wind. As he stood wrestling his thoughts, a single snowflake drifted down and lit on his nose.

Where would he go tonight, if not with the madwoman? With Annie MacCallum, he hastily corrected himself. He'd spent enough cold nights along freezing roadways.

She stood quietly awaiting his answer, the feather on her hat shivering in the wind. Her dark eyes watched him with care, holding an unreadable expression.

Was it something in those eyes that convinced him? Tam did not know, but suddenly it felt as if he stepped beyond himself, right out of this weary, hungry body with its mangled hand.

"Well, then, Annie MacCallum," he told her, "let us go and see the priest."

Chapter Two

She had done well, Annie thought as they walked across the market square toward the kirk, far better than she'd expected when she first climbed the steps of that platform. Despite the fact that it had taken her nearly all day to screw up her courage and make the announcement, despite the way her knees had trembled with terror when she clambered up and how her voice croaked when she forced it out, she'd accomplished her goal.

She stole yet another look at the man who walked beside her and wondered if he noticed her knees shaking even now. Could he tell how terrified she was, or had her determined self-possession masked her uncertainty? She knew very well she rarely displayed her inner turmoil, no matter what she felt.

But oh, aye, she'd done well. He was very nearly perfect aside from his hand, and one could not have everything. Indeed, even there fate had been kind to her. If not for the injured right hand, the fingers of which were twisted into a stiff claw, he'd surely have been hired by someone else at the outset and unavailable to accept what he clearly considered her mad proposition.

She could see his opinion in his eyes, and fine eyes they were, too—clear gray as the sky on an autumn morning. The color of his hair also reminded her of autumn, the warm brown that oak leaves turned before they fell. At the moment, he wore a scruffy beard that obscured the lower half of his face, but she found his nose, straight and proud, pleasing. Well set up, he topped her considerable height by a good bit, the strength of his body quite apparent despite his ill-fitting, ragged clothes.

He is not meant to please you, lass, she reminded herself sternly. *Not as if this will be a marriage in truth, or you will sleep with him*. Aye, for she had learned better; no man would set limb in her bed. Tam Sutherland would be a hireling in all but name.

Still it went to show, when one fastened one's faith upon a course and held to it despite doubt and trepidation, rewards came. For he was the perfect age: not too old and yet not a sapling. The odious Ned Randleigh might just consider him a proper mate for her.

That was, if Ned Randleigh thought anyone a likely mate for her. But aye, she meant to present Randleigh with a *fait accompli* when next he came calling.

At the edge of the market square, Annie paused. "That is my wagon there. Wait but a moment; I maun collect my lad."

Sutherland looked at her in surprise but said nothing. Good—he was not the sort to spit out his thoughts before he contemplated them. Better and better, for she could tolerate many things save a quarrelsome, overbearing loudmouth in either servant or husband.

Snow had just begun to gather on the cart. Old Rake turned his head to look at Annie and bared his teeth in what looked more grimace than smile.

Sorry, my good fellow, she told him silently. *We shall be moving soon.*

Jockie, as she expected, huddled not in the cart but under it. He came scrabbling out at her approach and began gesturing and mewling at her.

"Aye, lad, I am that sorry I took so long. We are going now to the kirk. Will you lead Rake?"

Jockie gibbered and nodded, caught Rake's harness by the cheek strap, and turned the old horse round.

By now the square lay full of fluttering snow and darkness. For an instant, Annie thought her newly chosen husband had gone just like the drunk, and her stomach sank. Then a shadow shifted and she saw him waiting, solid in the gloom.

"Come," she told Jockie again, in an effort to discipline her sudden rush of gladness. "Meet your new master."

****

Tam Sutherland's reaction to Jockie, so Annie supposed, would tell her much about him, as people's responses to the lad always did. Many folks crossed themselves or made the far older sign against evil. Some threw stones. Ned Randleigh always ordered him off as if he did not want to look at him, but Jockie, bless him, never went.

She reassured herself again; as soon as tonight she would have a barrier between herself and the vile Randleigh.

She watched Sutherland carefully as they approached, Old Rake wheezing in the cold air. She caught Jockie by the shoulder and gently drew him up beside her. Jockie hated meeting people, and who could blame him?

"Jockie…" She spoke in the quiet tone that usually served to calm the lad. "This is Tam Sutherland. He will be my husband and thus your master."

She felt Jockie's reaction through her fingers. With a grunt, he flinched and tried to pull away, then bent his head. Tam Sutherland's face became a study of surprise, wonder, and at last, consideration. Would he spit? Withdraw? Annie narrowed her eyes and waited.

"Grand to meet you, Jockie," Sutherland said in a voice as soft as her own, and Annie's heart clenched and melted.

Very well, then, he had passed the first trial.

"Jockie has great difficulty speaking," she told Sutherland carefully. "But he does manage to express his wants, do you no', lad?"

"Aye, and what of the horse?" Sutherland asked with what might be amusement. "Does he make his wants known also?"

"Right now Old Rake wants to go home." As did Annie, in truth. But not just yet. "Come along, Jockie. Father Alban will be waiting for us."

Jockie shrank back to Old Rake's side. Sutherland fell in beside Annie as they began moving.

In a low tone he asked, "This marriage you ha' in mind, will it be legal wi' no banns being read?"

"Father Alban is an old friend of my uncle, and I ha' spoken to him of this. He will accommodate me."

"Aye, and what will your uncle think o' this scheme of yours?"

"Very little, I imagine. He is dead."

Sutherland contemplated that without comment.

St. Lyon's church loomed ahead, appearing all at once out of the swirling snow. Annie turned to Jockie.

"You lead Old Rake round back and join us inside where you can get warm, eh?"

Jockie nodded and clattered off.

Annie turned to Sutherland and looked into his face, only to be struck again by how handsome he looked. But that had naught to do with anything, and she could not let it sway her good sense, not when she'd come so far.

"Before we go inside, I want to be sure I ha' your understanding. This is no' an ordinary marriage but something more in the manner of a hiring, which is why I came to the fair in the first place."

He inclined his shaggy head toward her slightly. "A hiring wi'out wages. That is against the law, you do ken."

She swept him with her gaze. "And are you a man to adhere to arbitrary laws? I confess, I did no' get that impression."

"And," he returned, "are you a woman who needs to hire a husband?" He echoed her. "I confess, I did no' get *that* impression." He returned her stare, slow and attentive. "You are certainly bonnie enough to snare a husband the usual way."

To her surprise, Annie felt a wave of heat course through her. "I do no' want a usual kind o' husband. I want one who will tak' my orders and stay clear o' my bed. Be sure you are that man before we go inside and speak these vows."

One of Sutherland's eyebrows quirked up. "I was right at the outset; you are mad."

"So we ha' already determined," Annie agreed, beginning to grow edgy again. What if he refused at this late moment? Where would she find a substitute, with the market now deserted and the snow falling? Besides, she discovered she did not want a substitute; for reasons she did not quite understand, she wanted this man and no other.

"There is a story behind this," he said mildly. "I confess, I would like to hear it."

"Perhaps you shall, but not now—there is no time." Annie drew a breath and sought to deny the fear rising inside her, the fear that he might walk away from her after all.

But that curious smile crossed his lips again.

"Are you coming wi' me?" she pressed.

"It seems a damned clever way to secure the services of a farm worker whilst paying no wages," he said. "But aye, for all that, I will come along wi' you."

Chapter Three

At the doorway of the church, Tam balked and caught Annie MacCallum's arm. Since watching her climb the steps onto the rough platform he'd felt like a man in a dream—or under a magical spell. But the light spilling out through the leaded windows of the stone kirk made him blink and come at least partially to his senses.

"Wait," he said.

She looked at him. He could see her more clearly now and noted feature after feature. Her face, all sharp angles, did not fit the usual definition of pretty—nose too pointy, cheekbones too stark. But Tam would defy any man not to notice her, especially given those clever, dark eyes that met his with a directness he could not help but admire.

His pulse sped, and he let go of her as if she singed his fingers. She would not want him touching her anyway, if all she said proved true.

"Why is it necessary for us to wed this night? Would it no' be better to go back to this farm o' yours, give it some time, and see how we suit?"

"I ha' not the time for that."

"'Tis highly irregular, this," he said.

"I told you, Father Alban and I ha' come to an understanding. Exceptions the rules can be made, you ken. And Father Alban is very close to the bishop. I believe he can clear our way, if we pay a fee." Her lips curled. "When it comes to the kirk, Tam Sutherland, much can be accomplished by the proper application of a bribe."

"I ha' no coin."

"Do no' fash yourself. I will pay the fee."

"But," he protested helplessly, "will such a marriage stand?"

"Do you care?" she challenged. "What is this to you, save a job?"

"'Tis more." How could a man consider tying himself to such a woman as this, even superficially, without it meaning something?

"Father Alban will ask you a few questions, whether you are already married and such. You are not?" Her dark gaze sharpened.

Tam shook his head.

"Well then, he has assured me the joining will be legal, if a bit irregular."

A lie of a marriage, Tam thought, executed on the strength of a bribe to the kirk. Did he truly want to be in the midst of that? Did he want to continue roaming the Highlands devoid of a place to lay his head? The Devil whispered that question in his ear. And a place was a place, right? A hiring a hiring, even if the only wage should be the privilege of existing in this woman's company.

And, had he not prayed to get taken on at any cost?

"Do no' look so worried," Annie said. "This is not my parish or yours. When it comes to it, I am not even a Christian."

The door swung open and flooded them with light. Tam narrowed his eyes against the glare and saw a black-frocked priest, his head topped by a snowy cap of hair that gleamed like a halo.

"Ah," the priest said. "I thought I heard you, Annie MacCallum. Come in."

The madwoman seized Tam's hand—his bad hand for all that—and towed him in. A scent of old incense combined with dust greeted him, but no warmth. The interior of the church felt as cold and damp as the outdoors.

The priest shut the door and turned to look at them. Tall and rail thin, he possessed a pair of piercing blue eyes and, at the moment, an expression of extreme dismay.

Severely he told Annie MacCallum, "I hoped you would reconsider this ill-advised intention of yours." His gaze flicked to Tam. "But I see you have found someone."

"Aye, indeed. Let us in, Father, and keep your word. I ha' sent Jockie round back, but he can stand as witness if needed."

The priest grimaced. "Why not? Witnesses to a marriage are required to be competent, but in this case I find it entirely appropriate."

"So long as the marriage will stand." To Tam's eye, Annie MacCallum still appeared calm. Yet her dark eyes glittered, and a feverish flush now stained her cheeks.

Father Alban sighed. "Come along; let us take a look at the prospective bridegroom."

Again Tam nearly balked. He wanted to grab hold of events and slow them down so he had time to think. What was the meaning of Annie MacCallum's words, saying she was no' a Christian?

Yet the priest had turned his back and led them into the church proper, down a center aisle toward the altar. St. Lyon's was not a large church and, at the moment, stood empty of everyone but them.

When they reached the altar, Father Alban turned to face them. Not unkindly he asked Tam, "My son, what is your name?"

"Sutherland. Tam Sutherland."

"And do you understand in full what this woman, Annic MacCallum, asks of you?"

Well, now, there was the question. Cursed if Tam did. But he could scarcely stand here before the priest and admit so.

"Aye."

Father Alban looked surprised. "And you come here freely anyway, without persuasion?"

"I do."

Annie MacCallum still clutched Tam's bent fingers in her hand, and a warmth had started gathering there, fighting the chill. It crept up Tam's arm, tingling as it moved.

Father Alban appeared perplexed. "How old are you, son?"

"Twenty-five last December."

"And you have not been and are not now wed?"

"I have no'. I am no'."

"Do you mean to take these vows honestly, solemnly, for life long?"

Did he? Startled, Tam's gaze flew to Annie MacCallum. She watched him as a crow might its prospective dinner.

Aye, and what would he do with his life, if he did not join with this woman? Homeless and without living

19

family, cast upon the world with no hope of making his way, he might well look on Annie MacCallum's offer as a Godsend.

But to take her for wife solemnly before that same God… He looked at her again, tracing each feature, noticing for the first time the hair peeping out beneath the wide-brimmed, green hat. He'd expected it to be as black as her eyes, despite her white skin. But the waves he saw pressed against her cheek looked a deep, rich brown.

He should call on his common sense, ask a thousand questions beginning with why she wanted this marriage so much. Instead, his tongue moved of its own accord. "Aye; I take these vows most earnestly."

And what did he see in Annie MacCallum's eyes? A flash of relief?

Father Alban grunted. "One as mad as the other," he muttered. "Tell me, Tam Sutherland, why would you agree to such an undertaking as this rather than hire on in the district like any honest man?"

Tam gently freed his fingers from Annie MacCallum's grip and held them before the priest's face.

Father Alban exhaled gustily. "I see." He turned his piercing gaze on Annie. "And this man will suit your needs? Solve your problem?"

What problem? Tam wondered, even as Annie MacCallum nodded.

"Well, then—I did promise your uncle on his deathbed I would aid and protect you in any way I might. Jockie is in the yard, you say? Let me fetch him and my housekeeper to serve witness."

He rushed off; Tam and Annie MacCallum were

left standing together in the flickering light of the altar candles.

"What problem am I meant to solve?" Tam asked her. "I believe I should know before we do this thing."

She hesitated. "I need the status of *wife*, you see."

"I am afraid I do no'."

"You see, back where I live there is a factor—"

Tam's reaction, swift and visceral, tightened his stomach muscles and flushed his skin. *Fire, pain, a pair of merciless eyes, and a face he longed with all his heart to pummel.*

He said, "There are factors everywhere." Tossing folks out of their homes into the winter cold, even the sick, and breaking their hearts. "They are the curse of the Highlands."

"Aye. This one preys upon women who ha' no' the protection of a husband."

Tam wished he could feel surprised by that; he could not.

Eyes fixed on his, Annie told him earnestly, "I do need help on my place. There is much to do, and Jockie is limited in what he can manage. I ha' a female servant also, a wee lass, but 'tis a struggle for us. So this scheme came to mind." She paused. "I am no' mad, as you think, though I warrant I must seem it."

Wryly, Tam said, "Do you make a habit o' taking on the disadvantaged?"

"You ha' no idea. Quick, Tam Sutherland, before Father Alban comes back with the witnesses, give me your assurance—"

She seized him again by way of persuasion, caught one of his wrists in either hand. Warmth once more suffused him, far more beguiling even than her gaze.

Ah, little did she suspect that she had come to the wrong man if she sought protection, the very last upon whom she should rely…he who had so markedly failed in the past to protect those he loved.

The thought that he might have another chance, an opportunity to defend a woman such as this, who wore her confidence like that green cloak on her shoulders and looked strong enough to make her own way in the world, struck him like sudden desire.

Dare he hope, after losing all but his life, he might yet mean something to someone?

Chapter Four

Annie prayed she revealed none of the doubts that wracked her as she stood before the altar with Tam Sutherland, waiting for Father Alban to read the marriage service. All this day, through the endless morning and interminable afternoon, she'd focused on her intentions and kept control of her emotions, never allowing her composure to crack.

She could not allow herself to break now. If she did, she believed her bridegroom would bolt like one of the wild creatures she so often strove to assist, back home.

He had the same look in his eyes as they stood before the priest, with the two reluctant witnesses standing by.

Jockie muttered and gibbered to himself. Mrs. Davies—Father Alban's housekeeper—had made no secret of what she thought from the outset.

"Scandalous, this, Father!" she complained as soon as she came in. "I should refuse to be part of it. There is the bridegroom looking no better than a tinker in his filthy rags. And the bride!" She lowered her voice but not by much. "A witch. I am that surprised the roof does no' fall in on us. And," she added, as if it finished the matter, "no banns!"

Annie shot a startled look at Tam Sutherland when Mrs. Davies uttered that word—witch. She'd hoped to break the truth to him more gently. Yet he merely stood with a stunned look on his face, like a man who'd been stuck over the head with a rock. Had he even heard?

Now she strove to master her tripping heartbeat, which stirred the green fabric of her dress. She supposed she should at least listen to what the priest said as he began reading the service, though the actual rite meant little to her. It was not as if they stood handfasted and declared their union.

His mangled hand, stiff as a claw, all the fingers grown crooked. How would it feel to stand handfasted with such a man?

Halfway through the reading, two of the candles on the altar abruptly flickered out. Mrs. Davies caught her breath. A third candle gutted with a gout of smoke. Father Alban faltered in his recitation and looked at the offending taper nervously.

"I told you," Mrs. Davies breathed, her voice spectral in the gathering gloom.

But one candle yet burned; Annie noted it was the one standing farthest east—a significant sign to one such as she.

"Best hurry," she whispered to the priest.

He nodded. The end of the marriage service came with a rush; he reached out and joined Annie's hands with Tam Sutherland's, which made Annie start. Could this union hold any real meaning?

The priest wrapped his cloth around their hands and spoke the final words. Annie found herself clutching Sutherland's ruined fingers after all, cold as the air around them.

Father Alban gave a restrained smile. "The groom may kiss the bride if he does so wish."

Sutherland hesitated, his eyes asking Annie a question. Because Mrs. Davies stared and because she wanted all this done proper, Annie lifted her face to him.

He leaned in, and his lips found hers, warm and questing. The kiss should have been chaste, a mere mark of the occasion. Instead his mouth lingered on hers, the only heat in the chilly room.

Annie drew away, and he released her hands.

With a huff of disgust, Mrs. Davies stomped from the room. The final candle kept burning, leaping wildly in the draft Mrs. Davies left behind. By its light, Annie gazed into her new husband's eyes.

Her husband.

Oh, what had she done?

The only thing she could to protect herself. She acted at the spur of pure necessity. Did she not?

"There now," Father Alban said. "Come with me to sign the book. Jockie," he added, "go you to the kitchen, and Mrs. Davies will give you something to eat."

Jockie shuffled off. Annie followed Father Alban out the side door to his study, all too aware that her husband followed.

Her husband.

With a flash of warmth she relived the sensation of his lips on hers. If she felt any attraction for this man—any at all—she had better put it away from her. For this was not intended to be that kind of marriage.

A single lamp burned in the priest's study. By its light he drew forward a large book and opened it to the proper page.

"First," he said and picked up a salver which he

extended to Annie.

Bribery—a requirement of this world that proved just what a sham her marriage was. But, Annie reminded herself, it would bring her safety.

She looked down at her hands, each of which bore two rings, all of which had once been her mother's. She had nothing else with which to pay for dispensation.

And so she must choose among them even though each held deep significance. A small diamond in a heavy, gold setting; no, she could not part with that. An equally modest ruby, also on her right hand. On her left, a sapphire—the color of the sea, and a square-cut emerald, the color of the earth.

Ah well—she supposed marriage might be considered an earthly matter. Not allowing herself to hesitate, she drew the emerald ring from her finger and dropped it on the salver.

Father Alban withdrew the tray the way an adder might its tongue; a piece of her heart, nay her soul, gone.

In a modest tone Father Alban said, "I will make sure it reaches the bishop."

Tam Sutherland began to speak; Annie shot him a look, and he narrowed his eyes but fell silent.

"I also think," Father Alban went on, "you should stay here the night. It is late to be starting out on a journey. Plus you want this to seem as ordinary as possible. Jockie can sleep by the kitchen fire if he likes; I will ask Mrs. Davies to open one of the guest rooms for you."

One of the guest rooms? Aye, well, a newly wedded couple could scarcely ask to sleep apart.

"Fine, that," Annie said, again striving to conceal

the turmoil inside. "But Jockie will probably be happier sleeping near Old Rake."

"Sign the book, and we shall sort it all." Father Alban directed a look at Sutherland. "Can you write your name?"

Sutherland, now ramrod stiff at Annie's side, grimaced and shook his head. "No' with this hand."

Father Alban clicked his tongue. "I should have thought. Can you make your mark using the other hand?"

"Aye."

"Good enough, then."

Annie signed the book and passed the stylus to Sutherland, their fingers tangling as she did. Suddenly her knees threatened to fail her once more. She edged to a chair and sat down.

Sutherland's mark made, Father Alban took back the book and eyed Annie's new husband up and down.

"A bath is in order, I think, though Mrs. Davies will have my hide for putting her to so much work this late in the day. And shall I see if I can find some clean clothing?"

Sutherland looked down at himself and flushed a ruddy hue beneath his scruffy beard. Annie experienced an all-too-familiar rush of compassion—something she had not expected to feel in this situation.

His natural dignity, that which she had noticed at the outset and which shone from him despite his obviously wretched circumstances, overmastered his embarrassment. "I would appreciate that, Father."

"And then," said Annie, following the trail of her compassion, "perhaps if the payment I ha' made allows for it, Father, a small supper?"

Father Alban nodded. "Let me speak to Mrs. Davies."

He hurried off, leaving Annie and Sutherland standing alone in the soft light of the lamp.

"I am sorry," she said then. "I should ha' thought at once how hungry you must be."

He turned those fine, clear eyes on her and shrugged. Aye, and she had seen that look before, in the eyes of creatures that had been hard used over a long span of time. They shouldered the want the way they might a load. This man, so she could see, had shouldered much.

When he did not speak, she told him, "I hope you do no' mind staying here the night."

"No doubt wise." She liked his voice, soft and almost musical. "How far off did you say your farm lies?"

"About five miles due east." She reached up and took off her hat, feeling as if she removed armor. She had girded herself well for this day's work but could ease now, surely.

His gaze, resting on her hair, quickened, and she wondered what he thought of his bargain.

To distract herself from that question, she went on talking. "The place once belonged to my uncle, and my grandfather before him. My mother and I lived with my uncle many years after my father died. There is a good, sturdy house, and the land produced well when my uncle was alive, even though he was more scholar than farmer. Since his death…well, two women alone, we struggled to keep up."

He eyed her again, gaze lingering on the remaining rings on her fingers. "And does your laird tolerate the land failing to produce?"

Annie smiled wryly. "My uncle and the laird were good friends. It has bought us leniency up till now. But the laird no longer lives on the land, and his factor—a man called Randleigh—is harsh."

Sutherland's face contorted; for an instant murderous rage looked at Annie from his eyes. She felt a qualm, yet the anger departed as swiftly as it came. "A common story these days in the Highlands." The mild comment defied what lingered in his voice—hatred sharp as a blade.

She said gently, "Unfortunately that is true."

"And your mother, she is no' still wi' you?"

Now Annie's face contorted. "She died just over a year ago, in the winter. Took a chill, and I could no' save her." Not all her efforts or her prayers to the powers of fire, water, earth or sky had served to keep the spirit she most needed in the world with her.

"I am that sorry," Sutherland said softly. "'Tis a particular torment, watching someone we love die."

He sounded like a man who knew. Annie looked at him curiously, but before she could ask, Mrs. Davies came bustling in.

"Well, come along with you then. Making all this work for a body at the end of the day." She glared at Annie. "Mistress MacCallum, I ha' given you the room at the top of the stairs."

"Mistress Sutherland now," Annie corrected, and her new husband started.

Mrs. Davies snorted. "Either way, your supper awaits you in the kitchen, and you will get no better this night."

Annie did not doubt it.

Chapter Five

Tam cursed softly as the razor, scraping across his whiskers, took off another flap of skin. Of all the things he regretted not being able to do with his maimed hand, shaving ranked high.

He should just let the scruffy beard stay, he thought, peering into the wavy mirror with which he'd been provided. Yet the housekeeper, Mrs. Davies, had complained so vociferously and eyed him so disdainfully, as if he truly were the tinker to which she likened him, he wanted to make a good job of it. When she gave him the razor with a pointed look, he took up the challenge.

At least he felt clean—truly clean—for the first time he could rightly remember. Jockie had helped haul all the water and stood by now, waiting to empty the copper tub. At first Tam had been disconcerted by his presence but decided he had bigger problems than wondering about the odd servant.

Such as a wife.

He frowned at himself, and the razor slipped again. Over the last months he'd learned to do many things with his left hand, but fine tasks still defeated him.

A garbled jumble of words came from the door where Jockie hovered. The lad came forward at a sidle and held out his hand.

"Eh?" Tam returned.

Jockie shook his fingers at Tam impatiently. Surely he did not expect Tam to surrender the razor to him, allow this fellow to wield it so near Tam's throat?

When he did not hand over the implement, Jockie made a series of gestures to his own face, miming shaving. Then he pointed to Tam's maimed hand and shook his head.

Tam hesitated. "Nay," he decided then, "I think I will struggle on mysel'. But thank you kindly for the offer."

Not until Jockie returned to the door did Tam realize that beneath his wild mop of nearly white-blond hair, Jockie's own face looked perfectly shaved.

****

And so it seemed they were meant to share a room this night. Tam, standing in the hallway at the top of the stairs where he'd been directed, hesitated before the closed door.

He had stalled as long as he could, helped Jockie empty the tub, fussed with the clean clothing he'd been given out of items no doubt collected for the poor.

Aye, well, he reminded himself, I am the poor now.

At last Mrs. Davies had ordered him up the stairs, saying, "I canno' go to my bed until you get to yorn."

And now what? Did one knock at the door of one's own chamber? Perhaps so, in these circumstances. He rapped, feeling foolish.

"Come away in."

The room, small and barren, contained only a bed and a chest pushed against one wall. Tam barely noticed, all his attention snared by the woman who stood at the center of the chamber.

She had shed the green cloak—it hung from a hook

on the wall—and loosed her hair, which flowed down her back in a tumble of warm brown waves. Half turned away from him, she looked over her shoulder when he entered, and her eyes went wide with surprise.

Aye, and he had forgot his own transformation; he must look a different man. He felt it with food in his belly and clean clothes on his back.

His ma would be scandalized at how low he'd sunk—but he could not, dared not think of her.

"Master Sutherland."

Carefully he closed the door behind him. "You had better call me 'Tam,' had you not? Since we are…"

"Wed." The word gusted from her. "'Twill take some getting used to, that."

He nodded.

"And, Tam, have you regrets over what you ha' undertaken this day?"

He ran his gaze over her slowly, from the top of her glossy head to the front of her green dress, which trembled visibly with her heartbeat, and on down over her long legs outlined in the green fabric. He must have regrets, aye, but looking at her he forgot them.

His wife. He experienced a sharp surge of emotion. What if they had truly been destined for the same bed?

Because she eyed him so closely, he shook his head and raised his good hand to his chin. "I attempted to shave. Likely no' a wise decision."

She smiled faintly, an acknowledgement of his wry words. "You look…fine. Well." Tearing her gaze from him she glanced around the room. "This is a mite awkward, is it no'? To be truthful, I did not expect Father Alban to offer us lodging."

"I will sleep on the floor." He spoke it as an

absolute, and she did not quarrel.

"Very well so, but you will have some of these blankets. 'Tis no' warm in here."

True; the room felt almost as cold as the kirk.

"Good thing," she emphasized, "we sleep in our clothing."

"Aye. You might also wish to wear your cloak. 'Tis a fine piece, that." He nodded at it where it hung.

She smiled again. "It belonged to my mother." She hesitated as if she would say more, but turned to the bed, where she gathered up blankets and a pillow.

He wanted to tell her how lovely she was, how bonny her hair, and that he'd never seen a woman to match her anywhere in the world. But they were not words a man gave to a woman he scarcely knew, wife or not.

She handed him the armful of blankets. "I hope you will be warm enough."

"I ha' slept in worse places."

Her gaze met his. "As you said, there is a story in it. You will have to tell me sometime."

He nodded again and looked about for a place to spread his bedding in the small chamber. At last he made a nest between the bed and the wall, far nearer than he liked to the place she would lie.

"Tell me when I may blow out the candle," she bade.

"You may."

"Good night."

The room went dark, and Tam heard the ropes on the bed creak as she climbed in from the other side. Settling his weary bones, he tried to get comfortable. His hand always began aching at night for some reason and disturbed his sleep.

This night, though, it might well be his thoughts that kept him awake. He lay in the dark, eyes wide, and wondered why she trusted him here with her. Did she not fear he might rise up in the night to rob her, take the rest of those rings from her narrow fingers, and flee? He might do that and easily. He might also force himself on her there in the bed with none to say him nay, and him her husband. He would not, but she could not know that.

How dared she trust him?

Ah, and had he forgotten she was a madwoman?

He turned on his side, seeking comfort, and heard her move also. What had he done, tying himself to her even if only in name? Well, but since that awful night back home, his life had not counted for much.

Like as well throw in his lot with a madwoman as anyone else. And she did not seem harsh or cruel, which counted for much, as his ma used to say.

He shut his mind to that—pushed the memories from him once again—closed his eyes, and prayed for sleep.

Chapter Six

"We are nearly there." Annie glanced once more at the man beside her. She wondered, not for the first time, what he would think when he laid eyes on her home.

He'd spoken little during their journey, which, prey to her thoughts, she found overlong. Old Rake never moved quickly—the ancient horse tended to find his own pace. They might almost have been able to walk faster, yet the three of them rode, Tam and she together on the bench and Jockie behind.

Surprisingly, when they set out, Tam asked Annie for the reins. He managed them competently with his left hand; the right he kept tucked inside the front of his jacket as from the eyes of the world, though it may have only been an effort to avoid the cold. The day proved sharp, though the snow had flown and they traveled beneath a windswept blue sky.

"There, now—this is the track."

To be sure, the old horse knew the way and veered right of his own accord. The narrow lane always made Annie think of a tunnel, even when the enclosing trees showed very little green. She felt the magic of the place begin to nibble at her, along with love for those she'd left there.

Tam's face went still. She stole yet another look at him. How handsome he looked with the rough beard cleared away—despite all the nicks. He possessed a typically Scots face with lean cheeks and stark cheekbones, a noble forehead and strong chin. His well-proportioned nose put her own sharp beak to shame and his brows lay level over those clear eyes.

Yet the countenance revealed little enough of what he thought, save when she surprised him. She did so now by touching his arm.

"Have a mind for the animals."

Upon the words, a flurry of barking broke out, and Ruff flew up the track toward them, with Ella struggling behind. In the back of the cart, Jockie set to mewling. He let himself over the side and shuffled ahead to greet the dogs in mid path.

Old Rake halted and stood blowing as if he'd just run a race. For him, the five-mile journey likely seemed one.

"What—?" Sutherland began to speak before astonishment silenced him; she watched those handsome eyebrows soar.

Fiona, the hind, came prancing down the trail, placing her three remaining hooves carefully. The two goats, Ban and Dubh, followed her as usual, and Annie imagined Mairi the fox watched from somewhere close by, if hidden.

Sutherland stared from the trail, where both dogs leaped about Jockie happily, to the approaching menagerie to Annie's face.

"What is this, then?"

"They live here, all of them, with me. Most found their own way or were brought here, injured. There were others I could no' save. We have the usual farm beasts, as well, mostly in the byre."

Tam blinked as the doe picked her way carefully around Jockie and the two dogs to press her delicate nose into Annie's lap. Annie stroked her soft head before leaning out to bestow similar caresses on each goat so they would not feel slighted.

"Are they all damaged in some way?" Tam asked.

"Not all, but most. Fiona, here, was caught in a snare. Both goats were abused by their last owner, as were the dogs. Ruff, as you can see, carries the scars of his beatings. He may be afraid of you for a time, until he grows used to you. He fears most men. Wee Ella had her ears cut off." She caught her breath and turned to look full in his face. "I tell you now and true, I canno' abide cruelty. I will tolerate many things from you. Not that."

He nodded slowly before his lips tightened. "You seem to collect misfits, mistress." He held his ruined hand up in front of her. "Do you not?"

About to answer, Annie instead warned, "Och— look out."

The large brown form, utterly silent, swooped at them; Tam ducked just in time to avoid a bump on the head.

He swore and raised his arms to defend his face.

"Nay," Annie bade, "he will no' hurt you. 'Tis but Sol—the owl."

"By God!" Tam lowered his arms and peered at the bird, which lit on the bough of a tree. Fervently he added, "By all that is holy!"

"Aye." Annie smiled into his face. "All here is most holy."

****

Tam decided he had been right at the outset. The

woman was mad, and her dwelling twice so. The house itself, as he saw when they at last cleared the beasts from the road and prodded the old horse into moving again, proved no more than an overgrown cottage built of stone on stone, with a thatched roof that looked in need of repair, and ivy everywhere. Trees bent overhead, lending it shelter, most of them rowans and pines.

And everywhere he looked, he saw animals: hens pecking in the yard, any number of cats, a cow grazing near the hedge, and a hare that, curiously, the cats and owl all let be.

The owl accompanied them on their way and, to Tam's horror, flew into the house through a side window, which stood open. To further add to the confusion, a girl came out of the house door, wiping her hands on her apron.

"That is Sonsie," Annie informed him even as she swung down from the cart. "She—"

Any explanation broke off as the lass reached them; Tam gazed into her face and saw she had a hare lip, one of the worst he'd ever beheld.

No longer able to feel surprise, he nodded to her, even though she stared at him in outrage.

Sidling up to Annie, she cried, "You went through wi' it, mistress? Indeed, I canno' believe it."

"Aye well," Annie returned, "believe it, for there he stands—my husband, Tam Sutherland."

"Wed? Sure and true?"

"Sure; I am no' so certain about the true."

The girl, for Tam supposed her no more than fourteen, lowered her voice. "You bribed the priest?"

For answer, Annie held out her hands, revealing

one of the rings missing.

Sonsie gasped. "But, your dear mother's ring…"

"What was I to do?" Annie glanced about the yard. "Pay Randleigh's price?"

"Nay, never." Sonsie turned a pair of shrewd hazel eyes on Tam. "What manner of man is he?"

"That we will all learn together. Come now, it has been a long journey for poor Old Rake. Let us get him inside."

"I can do that." Tam stepped forward and started unfastening the horse's bridle. He saw Sonsie's gaze fall on his hand. She said nothing, but he felt compelled to answer that stare all the same.

"I am no' so hampered I canno' earn my keep. Wee lass, if you will be kind enough to show me his stall, I will give him a good rubdown."

Sonsie hesitated and looked at Annie, who nodded.

"Come, then," the lass said. "Mind the creatures."

How could he do otherwise?

Sonsie led him away, and he saw a fine stone byre at the back with a wide-open door. Aye, the place might be better appointed than many he'd seen, yet as a working farm it appeared sorely lacking. Of course, according to what Annie told him, they had been two women alone after the death of her uncle.

He straightened his spine. Happen he could salve his pride by proving useful.

They rounded the house, and he asked, "Tell me, Miss Sonsie, did I truly see a wild owl?"

"Nay, a tame one. Sol was shot by an arrow, and Mistress Annie nursed him back to life. Now he will no' leave her."

"But—he went into the house."

"Aye, so?"

Tam swallowed. Back home their stock had shared the croft house in winter, penned at one end. But his ma would have fainted if a great bird like that moved in.

"The other animals, do they come and go at will also?"

"The dogs do, some of the hens, and the cats. Most the others sleep outside or here in the byre. 'Tis a fine, big byre, as you can see."

It was, and reasonably clean inside, the stalls filled with deep straw. Old Rake wandered into his box without persuasion. Sonsie pointed out the combs and left them together.

"Well, so," Tam addressed the big horse as he began to curry him. "Such a place I ha' landed mysel'."

Old Rake rolled an eye at him, and Tam, figuring the horse liked the sound of his voice, went on. "Do only damaged creatures come to her, then?" Those like him. And so, had it been fate that directed him and Annie MacCallum together?

Annie Sutherland now—he had to remember that.

"And," he went on to the horse in order to expand that thought, "were you in need o' saving also?"

He discovered the answer to the question as he worked, finding long, hard ridges crisscrossing the horse's back and flanks, where someone's whip had cut deep.

"There now, old fellow," he crooned, "and who would do that to you?"

"His former owner." The answer came from the door of the byre. Tam spun to see Annie standing there. "Parsimonious old fool took no note of Rake's age and beat him because he would no' work fast enough."

Tam slanted a look at her. "How did you come by him?"

"The man's wife brought him to me at the dead of night and in tears. Said she could no longer abide watching her man take out his spleen on the horse, and Rake so mild-natured. He is that too, for all his size." She went on before Tam could speak. "I like the way you do that—so gentle over his welts. Rake likes it, too. Just look at him."

"Easier than shaving, this." Tam smiled. "Sometimes the hand serves." He glanced about. "Will you wish me to sleep here? I do no' mind—'tis far better than where I ha' been laying my head."

She straightened. "Now, how would that look, my new husband sleeping in the byre?"

"How do ye want for it to look?"

"Right and proper—as if we are in love." Slowly she approached; when she drew near enough, she raised a hand to Rake's nose. "Do you think, Tam Sutherland, you can manage to pretend?"

"Pretend?" he repeated with a note of teasing in his voice. "Do you mean, like this?" He leaned in and kissed her, a far more chaste kiss than they had shared before the priest. But her eyes went wide. He smiled at her surprise and finished, "Why no' let me try and see?"

Chapter Seven

Night drew down with a chill wind that chased about the stones of the yard. Annie had spent the last of the afternoon showing Tam Sutherland about the farm with Jockie in tow. Tam's guarded expression revealed little of what he thought, but she did not suppose he approved of the creeping neglect that plagued the place.

He spoke only once, when they surveyed the back fields. "But what do you grow?"

"Turnips there, potatoes, and usually some barley. Beets also and, of course, kale."

"Does it pay your way?"

Annie smiled at that, the continual refrain of the true crofter. "You are a farmer," she guessed.

"Used to be, before—" He turned his head and looked square into Annie's eyes. "We were cleared, up north. My parents did no' survive the eviction."

"Och, I am that sorry. Was that when you injured your hand?"

"Aye." For an instant, agony stared at her from his eyes, but he buttoned his lip and said no more.

Now she felt glad to be at her fireside with everyone for whom she cared gathered near—Sonsie, stirring the stew she had made, Jockie come in for his dinner before going to the byre where he preferred to sleep, both dogs, and Glen, the house cat. And of course Sol, perched on the branch Annie had fitted for him.

And Tam. Well, no—she did not care for him. *Yet. Despite that kiss in the byre.*

Would she, ultimately?

A terrifying question, that. When she'd conceived this idea of procuring a hand who might also fill the role of husband and so act as a buffer for her, the prospect of affection had not come into it. She'd imagined someone sturdy and most likely taciturn—utility in two boots.

She should have known better, she thought now, eyeing Tam by the firelight. She should have understood herself better, for she grew attached to everything, from wounded rabbits to ailing badgers, no matter how difficult they proved.

And, she had to admit, Tam Sutherland had not proved difficult so far. Instead, with his gentle hands—even the one hampered—his wry humor, and his forbearing nature, he looked to fit into the life here as she would never have dared hope.

Quite likely shocked by the things he'd seen today, he had not declared it. Sometimes his brows flew up; once or twice he rubbed at his chin. But if he had an opinion, he kept it to himself.

Not a cruel man. Annie smiled a bit. The very best thing he could be.

She watched him now as he took his place at the big scrubbed table, keeping an eye all the while on Sol, where the owl sat on his perch. Sol's presence seemed most difficult for Sutherland to swallow. Indeed, even as Annie took the seat opposite him he leaned in and asked, "Does the bird stay indoors all night, then?"

"Well, aye."

"Does he no' go out to hunt?"

"From time to time. He canno' fly far, though as you saw, he can fly. The arrow damaged the muscles of his chest, and he has very little strength."

Tam eyed the owl, and Sol stared back at him impassively.

Sonsie, having served everyone, sat down and stared at Annie's hands, which rested beside her plate. "I still canno' believe you gave away your green ring."

"Needs must, Sonsie," Annie said, not wishing to discuss the matter.

Sonsie's small face wrinkled in distress. "But 'twas your mother's. What would she say?"

"I am certain my mother would understand."

"Well, I do no' like it." Sonsie glared at Tam. "Does no' seem like a fair exchange to me."

"Come now." Annie struggled for a light tone; sacrificing the ring had gone hard with her. "A bauble like that can no' help out around the place, canno' curry Old Rake or haul water from the well or bring in the harvest."

Sonsie insisted, "But 'twas part of her, and we will never see it again."

True, Annie acknowledged silently, pain flaring in her heart.

Jockie mumbled words around his stew, and Tam withdrew his gaze from the owl to stare at him instead.

"Of course, you are right," Annie answered Jockie.

"Eh?" Tam inquired. "What did he say?"

Annie smiled at Jockie before she replied, "Only that my mother's spirit lingers near us, rings or no."

Tam glanced about the room as if he expected to see a ghost. Aye, he would suppose them all more than mad, if this kept up.

Sonsie sank into the gloom that had become habitual with her since the death of Annie's mother.

Sensing her agitation as he so often did, Sol fluttered about the room before returning to his perch, shedding several feathers in the process.

Tam turned his gaze on Annie. "Ah, so that is where you got the feather in your hat!"

Annie nodded. How could she hope to explain she'd worn it for luck and to keep those she loved near her?

And had it brought her luck in her choice of husband? Too soon to tell.

****

The evening meal finished, Jockie retired to the byre. Annie helped Sonsie clear away the dishes, and Tam went out to fetch a load of firewood.

Annie observed him from the corner of her eye to see how he managed—well enough. He made a cradle of his right arm, into which he piled the logs with the left, and stacked them beside the hearth.

Ruff also watched him, with open suspicion. But wee Ella followed him in and out, keeping so close to his feet she nearly tripped him more than once.

Annie waited for him to lose his temper with the little dog and kick her out of the way. If that happened, she told herself, she might yet put him out despite the high price of their wedding.

But he never did. Instead, when he finished ferrying the wood, he hunkered down and held out his good hand to the small animal.

Ella went to him without hesitation, which made Annie raise her brows and caused Ruff, always protective, to huff anxiously. Ella, who had been hurt so terribly by men, rarely went to them voluntarily.

She watched as Tam stroked her with the same gentleness he had offered Rake. An emotion she did not recognize stabbed her through the heart.

Ella pressed against Tam's knee, wriggling, and he caressed her mutilated ears. "Who would do such a thing to a bonny wee dog?"

"There is no explanation for the cruelty of men. I do no' ken who—or why. Ruff found her out on one of our jaunts, bound and tossed into the bracken."

Tam stared at her. "Bound?"

"Paws and muzzle, her poor ears still seeping blood. Left to die."

Darkness invaded Tam Sutherland's fine eyes. "Och, and sometimes I think there is naught but cruelty in this world. How can one hope to battle it?"

"With kindness," Annie declared. "With healing and faith." She caught herself up hastily; likely he did not want to hear her spout her passion. She nodded to the small dog who now pawed at his knee. "Sometimes it has its reward."

Sonsie did not appear convinced. She shot Tam a dark look before ducking her head at Annie. "May I go to my bed, mistress?"

"Of course, lass."

"Only I thought you might rather I sit up to keep you company." Sonsie shifted her eyes to Tam again.

Annie smiled. "I shall do well enough."

With yet another glare for Tam, Sonsie caught the housecat up in her arms and retired to her room. Annie and Tam, alone but for the rest of the animals and the fire, which on this cold night felt like another presence, eyed one another.

"You will have to tell me all their tales," Tam said very softly so Sonsie might not hear.

"The animals' or the humans'?" Annie inquired.

"Both."

Annie gestured to the settle before the hearth, and he joined her there. She leaned her head close, no more anxious than he for Sonsie to hear them speak of her. "'Twas my mother took Sonsie in. She was just a babe, born with that deformity you see. Her parents already had a passel of children, and when she came along her father would no' have her in the house. He insisted her mother put her in the heather to die."

"Just like Ella."

"Aye, like wee Ella. The woman could no' bear it and came to my mother, weeping. Most all the women came to my mother from time to time." Annie smiled bleakly. "Now they come to me, but I am no' a patch on her."

"What did your ma do?"

"Took the bairn in, of course. My uncle was still alive then—you should ha' seen him stare. But och, that poor wee mite! Uncle Dennis would no' gainsay my mother. He rarely did, though she turned his home into…well, more or less what you see."

"He must ha' been a rare sort o' man."

"He was. My father's brother, I often wondered if my father was anything like him, for I never knew my own da, not to remember, at any rate." She hesitated and added almost delicately, "I also wondered if Uncle Dennis were no' a bit in love wi' my ma. Though to be sure, there was never anyone for her but my da."

She shook herself mentally. "But you do no' wish to hear all that."

"I do." He gazed at her gravely. "If I am to find my place here, I need to know about those here ahead of me."

"You must think I ha' taken leave of my senses, hatching this scheme."

"I think you are very kind. And it must be a terrible hard job"—he nodded at Ruff beside her feet—"protecting them all."

Funny him understanding that, how difficult it had been for Annie to pick up the burdens her mother had seemed to carry so effortlessly. Annie sighed.

"What about Jockie?" Tam asked.

"Och, his tale is even worse. Some travelers came through the village many years ago now; they made their way by showing off curiosities. They kept Jockie in a cage and called him the Beast Lad."

"I am thinking your mother won him away?"

"Aye, with my uncle's help. My uncle was a man of some influence and a good friend of the laird, as well as Father Alban. Over the years since his death that influence has waned. And wi' the laird moved away—"

"Your situation has become perilous."

"Aye." She gazed at him. "You can see that I need a man here."

He glanced at his ruined hand ruefully. "And the best you could do was me."

"Nay." She longed to reach for his hand, to cradle it between hers, but did not dare. "I believe, given time, your presence will prove a good thing indeed."

A wonderful good thing.

Chapter Eight

Tam turned from banking the fire and caught his new wife combing out her hair, a sight that struck him like a blow to the chest. Aye, and what a picture she made, seated on the edge of the bed in the corner just in reach of the firelight, with the tresses flowing down her shoulders and back gleaming warm chestnut.

Unaccountably, Tam's heartbeat quickened. She wore a white nightdress, having changed while he tended to his needs at the wee house out back. She looked up from her task when he turned from the fire, her dark eyes glittering.

On his perch, the owl shifted. And from his place at Annie's side, Ruff glared at Tam. Should he make one wrong move, the two of them would likely rend him.

Aye and what move, wrong or otherwise, did he contemplate? Tempting a picture as she made, he could scarcely go and take her in his arms. She'd made it clear 'twas not that sort of marriage. She merely needed him as another fixture of this place.

So then what should he make of this feeling that rushed through him whenever he looked at her, the heat that started low down and flowed upward to his head?

"I shall just settle down here beside the fire, shall I?" he asked.

She stared at him, arrested. He felt her gaze move

over his body as if she traced that trail of heat. She shook her head.

"Nay, I think it best if you share the bed with me."

"Eh?"

She cleared her throat. "'Tis big enough, this bed. 'Twas my uncle's, and he was a big man."

That might be so but, Tam felt, was scarcely the point.

Before he could speak, Annie went on, "How will it seem if my new husband does no' share my bed?"

"Who will know?"

"The women who come to see me will question Sonsie. She is no' good at keeping secrets."

Tam edged closer to where she sat. "Will she no' let it be known you paid the priest a fee to join us?"

"Aye, but a donation to the kirk is no great thing." Annie laid her comb aside and clambered across the bed to the wall.

Tam swallowed hard.

"Best to take off your shirt and trousers," Annie bade.

"But—" That would leave him standing in nothing but his trews.

She smiled. "Blow out the light, if you are feeling shy."

Shy? It was not a description Tam usually applied to himself. He doused the light and shucked the clothing without glancing in her direction. The room still held a fair amount of radiance lent by the fire, all leaping shadows and brightness. Tam moved to the bed, and the owl ruffled his feathers; Ruff gave a growl that sounded like a grumble.

"Hush, Ruff," Annie said.

Ah, then, and did she want him right in under the covers with her? Cursed if he could tell, but he slid in anyway. She'd been right; the bed afforded enough room so that he could lie without touching her.

Ruff, still complaining, laid himself down at the foot of the bed. Ella jumped up on it, circled twice, and curled onto Tam's chest.

Annie laughed softly. "Do you mind?"

"Nay, I once had a dog, Gyp, who…" He paused abruptly as rage and hate suffused him. Because she listened, he choked the emotions back and concluded, "who would often sleep wi' me."

"Well, then."

She said no more, and peace settled around them even as the comfort of the bed stole in. Tam could scarcely remember when he'd last known such ease— or anything beyond anger, grief and despair. Who would have thought it would find him now, here, with this woman?

Such a curious woman she was. He recalled again seeing her yesterday morning for the first time, circulating through the crowd with the feather in her hat bobbing, and looking at him as if measuring his soul.

His eyes began to close; he'd nearly succumbed to sleep when she asked, "Does it hurt?"

"What?"

"Your hand."

It did, constantly—usually a dull ache that moved to sharp pain when he attempted to use the fingers.

"Aye."

"Here, let me see."

Before he could react, she slid closer in the bed and plucked his bad hand from his chest where it lay curled around Ella's small, warm body. Tam's breath caught as her fingers moved gently over his, soothing and stroking.

"Tell me what happened to you."

Her head now lay very near his on the pillow; her voice made barely a whisper in his ear. He could smell her scent, warm and beguiling, and her touch on his fingers both enflamed him and, strangely, deepened the sense of comfort.

"I…" His throat worked for a moment. He'd promised himself he would not speak of that night, did not even wish to remember it. The night he had failed those who loved and relied on him.

The irony of that struck him once again—for this woman thought to rely on him also. He should warn her, tell her she'd made a bad bargain. He should leave here before she invested more in him than just her mother's ring.

Leave, aye, come morning. For to save his life he did not think he could rise from this bed at this moment.

Meanwhile he should tell her how it had happened, how he'd failed. Give her fair warning.

"They had been threatening for months to clear us, you ken. The factor let it be known we could leave of our own will or be tossed out—our choice. But there was no real choice in it, for we had nowhere else to go.

"My da—my da had been born on that land; 'twas in his blood. He often said he'd sooner die than leave." Tam smiled grimly into the near darkness. "He had his wish after that. He'd been ill ever since autumn, see, wi' a cold in his chest. When they came, when it happened, they gave us no time to gather our belongings. He and my ma were both thrown out into the snow."

"But, your hand?"

She still massaged it, her touch a balm. Slowly she caressed and strove to straighten each of the bent fingers in turn.

"I tried to fight the men who came, but there were five of them—the factor and four of his men. When they broke the door in, I snatched up a cudgel, all I had within reach. They punished me for it, after."

"How?"

Tam narrowed his eyes. Despite trying to push it away from him, he had relived that scene a hundred times. What might he have done different? There must have been something.

"They dragged me outside. My parents were already there ahead of me, Da fighting for his breath and my ma scrambling in the snow. She was always such a proper lady, even if a crofter's wife. It hurt to see her treated like so much trash. Three of them wrestled the cudgel from me and held me down while the factor and his fourth man used their team to bring down the stones of the lintel so we could no' go back inside. My dog, Gyp, tried to defend me, but they clubbed him down with my own stick—dead." He swallowed convulsively, his throat suddenly too dry. "They set the inside of the croft house alight, everything we owned, while they held me down, and I could do naught to prevent it. Then they—"

Abruptly, he faltered before sucking in a deep breath and forcing the words from him. "They spread my hand on one of the stones and used another to crush it."

"By the powers!" Her fingers stilled on his, and he

felt horror crawl through her.

"After they rode away," he resumed unsteadily, "I ha' no time to think about mysel'. I helped my parents away up into the hills, looking for shelter."

"Could you no' go to a neighbor?"

Tam shook his head. "The factor—Cauldam was his name—let it be known that whatever household offered aid to those dispossessed would be next for clearing."

"Ah." She began stroking his fingers again, her touch tender. "And no doubt they all wound up being cleared anyway."

"Aye, eventually. It took some time. By any road, the long and short of it was my hand had no chance to heal properly."

"You saw no physician?"

He laughed incredulously in answer.

"Aye, well," she went on in a voice he imagined she used speaking to injured animals, "I may be able to do somewhat for it."

"You?" He turned his head on the pillow, seeking her eyes.

"Aye, I ha' the healing touch. Can you no' tell?"

"I can tell."

"I do no' ken that I can do much to make these fingers work again, but I should be able to ease the pain."

"How?"

"A massage just like this every day—"

Or every night?

"Perhaps twice a day, in the beginning. Do you feel any difference yet?"

"I do."

"Tam Sutherland, I am that sorry for the sorrow and grief you ha' suffered." Unexpectedly, she raised his mangled hand to her lips. He felt her mouth soft against his palm, blessing it with a kiss. "There, now, better get some sleep."

Damned if he could.

Chapter Nine

Tam awoke to find someone staring at him—several someones. The wee lass, Sonsie, stood not three feet away, glowering with open disapproval, her look mirrored almost perfectly by the owl on his perch. Neither of them blinked, and Tam could not decide which glare was the fiercer.

And the small white dog, Ella, stood on his chest regarding him also. Her expression, by contrast, denoted adoration.

Of his wife, though, he saw no sign; the bed beside him stretched empty and cold. He wondered if he had dreamed that conversation last night and the way she'd touched his hand.

He brought the offending member out of the blankets and scrutinized it. Still crooked and ugly, but it seemed to ache a mite less.

Ella licked his chin, and he shifted her gently so he could peer around her. He found Annie nowhere in the room.

"Where is your mistress?" he asked the scowling lass.

She sniffed. "Arisen long since and out about the chores of this place. 'Tis no' everyone can lie abed half the day."

No sooner had she spoken than the door crashed open and Jockie came limping in. Tam had noted last night how the lad rarely raised his head; now he did so, and Tam caught a good look at his expression, one of terror and dismay.

His crooked mouth opened and sounds issued forth, a series of mewling cries and a word. "Randleigh—"

"Sweet mercy forefend!" Sonsie exclaimed with equal horror. "And, foolish lad, did ye leave our mistress out there alone?"

Jockie spoke again. "Ruff."

"Ruff is with her? Well, that is something." She turned on Tam. "Get up! Make yoursel' useful."

"What—?" he began to inquire.

"'Tis the factor, Randleigh—the very reason you are here, as I ken full well."

Factor. The word caused a flood of anger to race through Tam's body. He shoved the bedclothes aside and got up all in one movement.

"What would the factor want here?" he wondered aloud.

Sonsie retorted, "You maun ken what he wants. Or did my mistress no' tell you whilst you were cuddling last night?"

Tam shook his head even as he seized his trousers and struggled into them. The honest fear in Sonsie's face belied her waspish tone. Barefoot as he was, he charged across the room and out the door, aware that both Jockie and Ella followed him.

He heard voices even before he emerged—one he did not recognize, along with Annie's strident crow-squawk, so different from her soft tones in bed last night. He saw her at once, standing in front of the yard gate as if she barred the way to the man who sat his horse beyond.

Regarding the man, Tam felt a chill chase up his spine following hard on the instinctive rage. Factors in the Highlands were not known for their soft natures. Neither were they usually men of the land they managed, too often brought in from England or the lowlands. Arrogance commonly marked them, but this man's countenance betrayed something that went beyond mere arrogance. His thin face looked greedy, his mouth cruel, and his hooded eyes were those of a predator.

"…expect me to believe…" he was saying to Annie when Tam appeared. The narrowed eyes switched from Annie to Tam, and the mouth, like a cut from an axe, slanted down.

"Here is my husband now." Annie's voice trembled, the only thing to betray her distress. For she stood foursquare, wrapped in her shawl, her hair still streaming loose down her back and Ruff at attention beside her.

A surge of protectiveness carried Tam forward across the yard to her side. When he reached her he heard the deep growl rolling low in Ruff's throat. He saw too that the factor came armed, a pistol at his side and a crop laid across his saddle. In his mind he could almost see the man felling the dog should Ruff decide to lunge.

For that reason, if no other, he nudged the dog aside and took his place at Annie's side.

She pressed close, and her hand snaked up his naked back; all a show for the factor's benefit, no doubt, but her action caused Tam's initial protective instinct to flare still more brightly.

He glared at the factor. "What is this?"

"This man is Laird Ardaugh's factor, Ned Randleigh. Master Randleigh, my husband, Tammas Sutherland."

Randleigh's nostrils pinched. "You did not tell me you intended to wed, mistress."

Annie's chin came up a notch. "I was no' aware I needed your permission."

"A bit sudden, this marriage, is it not?" The man's clipped voice betrayed him as English.

"Not at all. We were waiting only for the winter weather to break and so allow Tam to travel."

Randleigh eyed Tam up and down, for the moment not noticing his mangled hand which pressed into Annie's side.

Tam took an aggressive step forward. "And why should my wife's intentions be any business o' yours? She needed help on the place, and I ha' come. Henceforth, you will deal wi' me."

"Your *wife*," Randleigh emphasized, "knows full well that much of this district is slated for clearing— just as she knew the price of being passed over. I tell you as I tell her, that price still stands. Good day to you."

He drew up his horse with a vicious hand and turned from the gate. In a moment he had ridden off into the chilly mist that still clothed the hills and the trail.

The growl in Ruff's throat died.

Tam turned on Annie. "What does he mean? What price is this of which he speaks?"

She looked nearly overset with dismay. Her eyes, full of emotion, searched his, and a hectic flush rose to her face. "We canno' speak of it here. Come inside."

Tam refused to move. "Nay. You will tell me first."

Jockie, mewling in distress, approached them waving his hands.

"You are upsetting Jockie; he canno' abide raised voices."

"I ha' no' raised my voice," Tam pointed out. Perhaps, though, the lad sensed his ire, aimed at the man who had just ridden away.

He seized Annie by the shoulders and asked more softly, "What did he mean?"

She seemed to sag between his hands. "Come inside and I will tell you all."

****

Annie sat with her gaze fixed on her folded hands—much easier than looking at Tam, who sat opposite her. Their human companions had made themselves scarce, Jockie gone out to the byre to care for the beasts and Sonsie to the yard to feed the hens. At least some of the animal occupants remained. Sol still occupied his perch, watching over everything like a patriarch, and Ruff sat pressed to Annie's side.

She flicked one careful look at Tam's face, worried and stern.

When she did not speak, he urged, "Tell me about this man Randleigh."

"I already did. At least, I did say there was a factor."

"There always is." Tam twitched in his seat, and she thought of what he'd confided before they fell asleep last night. She shuddered inwardly with sympathy. Would he have come here, accepted the place she offered, wedded her, if he knew he strode straight into another such battle?

"He hails from England and was hired no' by our laird, a MacCallum true born, but his agents in Glasgow. He came here wi' a reputation as a hard man, but we had no idea at the outset what he truly was. So far he has cleared only a few—folks so behind in their rent none could say he had no' a legitimate reason. But he holds the threat of clearance over the rest o' us like a big stick."

"Where is the laird?"

"Gone to Edinburgh. They say he fell into debt and was forced to retire to a lesser holding in the city. To be sure, the big house stands empty now, save for Randleigh himself and a few servants." She gave a thin smile. "Sometimes I think Randleigh fancies himself the laird." She lifted her eyes to meet Tam's at last. "With a laird's privileges."

Tam cocked an inquiring eyebrow. "Meaning?"

"He has set prices for holding off on a clearing. From a family it might be coin—little enough per quarter, just what they can barely stand. But it makes the want in the district that much greater. There are children who did no' have enough to eat this past winter because of him."

"I see."

"Do you?" She leaned forward slightly, across the table. "From the women—widows and those no' yet wed, he demands a different price."

It took Tam a moment to grasp the truth. Annie could see when he did by the shock that flooded his clear, gray eyes. "Och, never," he breathed. "And they pay this?"

"Some do. Some are that desperate to keep a roof over their bairns' heads, especially during the winter. Some lasses have paid the price to keep their aging parents safe." She hesitated. "These women come to me for many reasons—for cures, for advice. One such, a maid before Randleigh interfered wi' her, now believes she is with child."

"Does the laird know this is going on?"

Annie shrugged helplessly. "He should, for I wrote to him. I do believe he received the first letter, though he did not reply. 'Tis hard to understand, that, for he was a good laird when he lived here, and fast friends wi' my uncle. I thought he maun act. I fear my second letter fell into Randleigh's hands, for he came and taunted me wi' the very words I had written. He told me then I did no' deserve to stay here, and he set his price. That was in the autumn. He said I maun pay by spring."

"So you went to the fair to get yoursel' a husband."

Her hand crept across the table to touch his. "I am sorry. I should ha' given you better warning that I dropped you into such a muddle. But I was that desperate."

"You could ha' paid him off as you did the bishop. Those rings…"

Annie's cheeks grew warm. "He would no' take any price from me but the one. I fear he has wanted that since he first rode onto this place." Annie could not imagine why. Perhaps he enjoyed the challenge of breaking her, for to be sure far lovelier women dwelt in the district.

"Aye, well," Tam said, "we will ha' to come up with a way to convince him he maun now stay awa' from you, will we no'?"

" 'We'?" She leaned still closer. "Dare I hope that means you are with me in this?"

He searched her face for a moment before he replied, "We are wed, lass, for better or worse. Surely that means I am wi' you."

Annie sagged with relief where she sat. "Thank you." She closed her hands on both of his. "Thank you, husband."

Chapter Ten

Tam stood in the yard and watched the sun sink into a bank of clouds to the west, marking the end of the day. He knew he should go inside to his supper; he could hear the clatter of plates and kettles from the house behind him. But the tangle of emotions in his heart bade him linger a moment more.

Aye, and he'd carried such a weight of feelings since the death of his parents—enough at times to turn his stomach. Anger, hate, self-doubt, and recrimination kept him awake nights. He should have done more to protect those who meant more to him than anyone in the world.

And now here he found himself called upon to protect someone once again—not the dearest in the world to him, granted, but who could fail to care for a woman like Annie, all courage and compassion? Already, with such perilous speed, he had feelings for her and those in her household.

Like the wee dog even now at his side. Ella quivered where she sat when he looked down at her, the sad remnants of her ears tucked close to her head.

What manner of person could do such a thing to a mere scrap of a dog, take a blade to its ears and cause it pain? What manner of man could press desperate, hurting widows and frightened maids for favors?

Nay, he did not blame Annie for the offer she'd

made at the hiring fair, or for bringing him here. But his feelings toward Randleigh were prodigious and frighteningly violent.

He had promised himself he would never care for anyone or anything again—the night his ma had curled up and died, still whispering his da's name, he had. His injured hand was his constant reminder of that, and of the fact that he'd failed them both.

How dared he suppose he could make a difference now?

Upon the thought, the house door opened behind him and Annie came out. He knew her by her step, the lightness with which she moved, and by her scent of mingled herbs and woman.

She paced to his side and laid her hand on his arm; Tam liked the way she touched him, with gentle warmth, and he remembered how it felt last night when she'd soothed his hand.

"Why do you tarry out here? It grows cold, and your supper is waiting."

His supper and her bed? Did that wait also? Might he expect her to touch him again, dared he hope for more?

He turned and encountered her eyes, alive as the night sky.

"I ha' been standing here thinking. About yon factor, Randleigh."

"Why spoil a lovely sunset thinking o' him?" Annie kept the words light, yet some of the brightness left her eyes. Aye, the man frightened her, and Tam suspected it took a great deal to frighten such a woman as this.

He drew breath. "When next he comes calling, I

mean to set him straight." Or, Tam thought, lie in wait for him and strike before any more arrogant words poured from the man's mouth. He found satisfaction in the thought, yet as he well knew it would serve little; another factor would soon be brought in.

Annie's fingers tightened on his arm. "Tam, I would not have you take any chances nor risks wi' your safety. I did no' bring you here for that."

"You wished for a shield, someone to stand between you and that blackguard."

"Aye," she admitted softly. "Mayhap I did. But…"

"Then you will ha' to let me stand in that place."

She studied him slowly, her gaze slipping from his face downward. Did it linger on his hand? Did she suppose him less than able to defend her as a man should?

But she said only, "Come awa' in. You will take a chill."

He nodded and turned, and wee Ella jumped up at his knee. When he bent to her, she leaped into his arms.

Annie laughed softly, the sound like bells in the gathering darkness. "You ha' a champion there."

"Aye, but yon Sonsie is no' so sure about me. I canno' tell what Jockie thinks."

"'Twill take time for Sonsie to trust you. Jockie is another matter. Speak to him. He can understand you, and if you try you will be able to understand him, as well. That may win his trust."

"And his mistress?" Tam stopped her with a touch on her shoulder. "Does she trust me also?" Enough to lie beside him again this night?

Once more she searched his eyes. For an instant he thought she might lean in and kiss him there in the dusky yard, and he wanted it so much he could barely breathe.

But she said, "I find I do, even though we are barely acquainted yet. That will mak' you suppose me as daft as you no doubt supposed when I climbed up on that platform at the fair. Aye, I saw the way you looked at me." She smiled. "I ha' an instinct about people, you ken. I am seldom wrong." She paused. "And I did notice you, from the first."

Ah, and what did that signify? What meaning that expression in her eyes? She had looked at him with interest, aye, the way a woman eyed a man.

Before she noticed his hand.

But ah, he could not suppose that made a difference to this woman who took in the maimed and the unwanted as a matter of course.

Ella licked his chin, and Annie laughed again. "Come you awa' in. We will worry about Ned Randleigh when he returns."

****

"Tomorrow is market day," Annie told Tam when both Sonsie and Jockie had gone off to bed and the two of them sat by the fire alone.

Sol had gone out to hunt, a rare enough thing. Annie tried not to worry about him; she did not like him going—it felt as if a small bit of her heart fluttered out into the night with him. And now, as she sat sewing before bedtime, she kept one ear cocked for his return.

Before bedtime.

She raised her gaze to study the man who sat at his ease opposite her, the firelight playing tricks with his features. Did he watch her from narrowed eyes? Did she capture his interest even as he captured hers? Did

67

he look forward to the moment they would retire to bed together, with any of the anticipation that had haunted her all this day? Aye, she longed for the warmth of his body beside hers, the unexpected delight of his presence when she woke in the night. A woman could right quickly get used to such comfort.

Ah well, she told herself, pausing her needle, had she not learned that each and every creature craved contact? And love. Should she be any different?

"Market day," he echoed when she said no more. "Shall you go?"

"Nay, but most of the men hereabouts do, and it gives their wives a small measure of freedom while they are awa'. Many of them come here to me."

"Oh?"

"They will begin arriving early—just so you are prepared and no' caught returning from the wee house wi'out your trousers," she teased.

"And why do they come to you?"

"Och, there are scores of reasons. Some bring their ailing bairns for a remedy. Some just come for advice. I read the cards for them, or the tea leaves."

Tam's eyebrows flew up. "Are you a seer, then?"

Annie stilled her needle once more. "I am no' the seer my mother was. She had the true Sight. I inherited just a part of her ability, but I would never withhold help from anyone."

He said nothing, and she eyed him still more closely, wondering what he thought. Most Highland towns and villages harbored at least one person recognized as a seer—the malevolent ones were called witches.

"They maun ha' faith in your cures," he said at last,

"if they keep coming."

"They have few choices. And they trusted my mother so have transferred that trust to me."

"What sort of advice do you give them?"

"The best I can. 'Tis none of it truly mine, you understand. The cards do speak, as do the leaves." She smiled slightly. "As for those who ask me to read the tea leaves, I am not at all certain whether they truly seek knowledge or just a few minutes' peace to enjoy the brew."

"And," he challenged, "what do the leaves say?"

"Many things." She hesitated. "They spoke of you."

"Did they!"

"Och, aye—whilst still I contemplated this mad undertaking. Though as so often happens, I did no' take their full meaning at the time."

"What said they of me?"

"Only enough to reassure me now." Her lips twitched. "I saw a hat right up near the rim of my cup—or, to be more exact, a *tam*."

He laughed softly, and it sounded fine and warm in the quiet room. Annie laid aside her mending and leaned toward him. "How is the hand? Let me see."

He extended it to her without question, and she laid it, palm upward, on her knee. As she had last night, and listening hard to the wisdom inside her, she stroked from the palm outward along the twisted fingers, gently attempting to straighten them one by one.

"Think you can mend that, do you?" he asked even as he had before.

"Nay; just make it easier to bear."

Something flared in his eyes, a look she had never

seen from any man. "Come to bed wi' me, Annie." He nodded at their joined hands. "You can work your magic there."

Annie's heart leaped into her throat, where it began beating a fast tattoo. What did he mean? That they should lie together side by side as they had last night, keeping one another warm? That she should soothe his hand and bring him comfort? Something more?

But that had not been part of the bargain struck at the hiring fair.

Bargains may be changed, she heard her mother speak in her mind. *Altered for the benefit of both. Daughter, do not shortchange yourself.*

She stumbled to her feet, both her hands still clutching his, and he came with her. They stared into one another's eyes an instant before he drew her toward him and into his arms. Annie found herself suddenly cradled against the hard strength of his shoulder, where she promptly melted.

"I had no notion I was wedding mysel' to a woman possessing magic," he said softly. "Though I should have, given all these creatures and the feel of the place. Do you mean to beguile me, Annie?"

That had not been her intention; she'd merely meant to hire a husband, straightforward and plain. But she'd not figured on Tam Sutherland, and now, with his heart beating so strong beneath her cheek and the warmth of his arms around her, she almost wished she could. She would enchant him, make him see her as beautiful, make him wish to stay with her.

Forever.

She tipped her face up to his. "I do no' possess that kind of magic."

"Aye, Mistress Annie, but you do."

And like the answer to her prayer, his lips descended on hers.

Chapter Eleven

For much of his life, Tam Sutherland had endured a close acquaintance with hunger. Food had seldom been plentiful on the croft, especially by the end of winter. And these last months as he made his way about the Highlands looking for work and a place to lay his head, his belly had been empty far more often than full.

But the hunger he felt now, with Annie caught fast in his arms, outdistanced all of it. Sharp and avid, it reached up from a well of need he'd not known he possessed, threatening to consume him—and her.

Aye, he had already kissed her—once in the kirk and that other time in the yard. But not like this, nothing like this.

A ravaging beast would be easier to restrain than this sudden storm of passion, especially because he could taste Annie's hunger as well, leaping up to meet his own. Her desire touched and tangled with his even as their tongues tangled, hot and vital as the blood in his veins.

The inside of her mouth, a cavern of sweet warmth, welcomed him without reserve. Her arms slid luxuriantly about his neck, and her fingers dove into his hair to draw him closer. Her body pressed trembling against his, such a perfect fit it had his pulse pounding in his ears.

His mind screamed at him for caution even as his

manhood, lower down, demanded daring. His ears listened to the soft sounds Annie made as he ravaged her mouth, alive for a hint of her willingness.

Instead she broke the kiss and drew away from him, not far. Her eyes sought his in the dim light. "Tam…"

"Let me carry you to the bed." Was that him speaking? It did not sound like his voice, all rough with desire.

She hesitated, her hands cradling his face, her gaze holding his as if she memorized what she saw there. "I do no' think—"

"There is naught wrong in it," he told her. "We are wed."

"Aye, so," she acknowledged in reply.

He dove for her mouth again, sure he could never get enough of such delight. He drank of her deeply before releasing her lips to say, "I am able."

"I do no' doubt it."

"Let me show you."

"But, but—Tam, I never intended it to be that sort o' marriage. And there is no going back from such a thing."

"Are we no' meant to bring one another comfort? What better comfort, on a cold night?" He'd had no idea he could be so persistent. He whispered into her ear, "Tell me aye, or nay."

He caught the shiver his words coaxed from her and chased up her spine. "Aye," she breathed. "But I never—I ha' never…"

"I will do naught you do no' wish. You may halt me anytime. Only let us gang to the bed."

When she made no further protest, he swung her up

in his arms. A few strides took them to the bed, where he laid her down with tender care.

"Take down your hair for me," he bade. "You ha' such bonny hair."

She froze for a moment, like a woman struck, before sitting up and feeling for the pins that confined her tresses. They fell one by one, thick and glossy, and Tam watched them swirl about her shoulders even as he began to unbutton his shirt.

A growl from behind arrested him. Ruff stood there with ears back and teeth bared.

"Hush now." Annie slid to the edge of the bed and addressed the dog. "I want this." Her gaze moved to Tam. "With my whole heart, I do."

****

And who would ever have thought, Annie asked herself a bit wildly, I would be lying in my uncle's big bed while a man undressed me slowly, as if time had ceased to exist and the night stretched before us unending? Especially a man such as Tam Sutherland, whose quiet strength spoke to her on a level so deep it shook her, whose lips wooed her like an irresistible song, who had deemed her bonny.

Cursed if he did not make her feel that way.

He'd finished removing his shirt after Ruff went to lie down. He still wore his trousers and, no doubt, his trews beneath, but his chest and shoulders lay bare, outlined in firelight.

Mangled Tam Sutherland's hand might be; the rest of him attained perfection in Annie's eyes. Indeed, had the powers she worshipped created a man for her liking, he might be just like this, with a lean torso well-endowed with muscle, no doubt earned in the typical labor of a croft, and just enough hair to make her fingers itch to touch. His strong arms lent a feeling of safety such as she'd never known, and he tasted like heaven.

But did she truly mean to go through with this?

And why not? As he said, they were duly wed. She'd meant to go to her grave untried, had in truth never expected any man—save, perhaps, the vile Randleigh—to desire her this way. Now she lay like an offering atop the blankets while the fingers of Tam's good hand—nimble enough for the task—dealt with her clothing. He removed her clogs; she heard them hit the floor one by one. He felt his way up each of her legs and rolled her stockings down one after the other. He bent his head and kissed her knee, a shocking caress.

A wild thrill swept through her body, from her curled toes through the depths of her belly and clear to her lips, which promptly yearned to feel his again. What would he do next? She could barely breathe for wanting to know.

Ah, another intoxicating kiss, during which his hand moved to her bodice. But the tiny buttons there defeated him. He broke the kiss and gazed into her eyes.

"Perhaps fate is against this after all."

No sooner had the words escaped his lips than a loud rattling came from the window. He froze, superstitious wonder flooding his eyes.

Annie laughed. "'Tis not fate, that, but Sol coming home." She scrambled from the bed and went to throw wide the shutters. The owl glided in and fluttered to his perch. She closed the shutters and turned back to the bed. For an instant longer she hesitated, asking a question within herself, receiving an answer.

"You have one good hand," she told Tam, "and I two. Between us, I do not doubt we can deal with any challenge, including these wee buttons." And she unfastened her bodice before letting the dress fall about her ankles and returning to the bed.

****

Tam stirred groggily on the pillow and the remnants of pleasure whispered through him once again. Like the echo of music it was, only far sweeter. Deep as comfort and twice as strong, it seemed to enwrap all his senses.

His mind groped for the proper word to describe what he felt and came up with the only one that fit: magic. Annie breathed it when she touched him; she had bestowed it when their bodies joined, and now it possessed him whole.

A woman of magic, his wife who spoke with wild creatures, read the future in a tea cup, and provided him a kind of warmth he had never imagined.

And did she now sleep, this wondrous wife of his? They lay entwined together in the big bed, both of them naked as born. Her head rested close beside his, and her breath tickled his cheek.

No going back from it, she'd said, and aye, she spoke true. He had done more than explore her lovely body and pluck her maidenhood this night. He feared he had also given her his heart.

That had not been part of the bargain either. He did not know that she wanted his ragged heart at all. Sweet kisses, aye. Maybe even this deep comfort. Beyond that, all she'd truly asked for was someone to stand between her and the factor, the protection of being his wife.

Or, anyone's wife. That knowledge came to him suddenly, chipping away a little bit of his newly-acquired peace. If not for the fact that she'd made her plea so late in the day and he had been left there still with his mangled hand, it could have been some other man with the place.

And then he would not be lying here with her, so warm, so blessed, feeling so complete, like a ship come into harbor.

He protested that idea inwardly—his heart did—and he moved in the bed. Annie roused instantly.

"Tam?" she murmured. "What is it? Do you ache?"

She caught his mangled hand between her fingers, and his whole body responded. Somehow he fought back the immediate waves of desire and lay quietly while she massaged and stroked him, only his breath quickening.

"It does no' hurt," he realized, in amazement.

"No?"

"You do no' understand, Annie; it always hurts, more or less. Has ever since it happened. But not now." He turned toward her in the bed. "Maybe loving you has healed me."

"Do you think so?"

"I do."

"'Tis a bonny thought, but I fear the pain will return come morning."

"We have hours before morning." Leaving his right hand between her fingers, he cupped her breast with the other. She caught her breath.

What miracles her breasts were, mounds of softness tipped with buds that rose to his touch and beguiled his tongue. He wished he could see her standing naked for him with all that glorious hair swirling about her.

"Beautiful," he murmured.

"What is beautiful?"

"This." He teased her with his thumb. "You."

She laughed softly. "My uncle used to call me 'wee crow' for my black eyes and my beak of a nose."

"Your uncle is no' here, and I will call you what I wish."

"What will you call me?"

Magic, the source of all desire, hopelessly beguiling. But he could say none of that and instead told her, "I shall be pleased to call you my bonny wife."

Chapter Twelve

"So 'tis true." Nellie MacLachlan leaned her head close to Annie's and lowered her voice even as her eyes followed Tam about the yard. "'Tis all over the district you ha' got yoursel' a husband. No one seems to ken where."

"We wed in Oban." Annie smiled to herself. Word had spread even more swiftly than she'd expected.

Nellie narrowed her gaze. "Well, he is a fine-looking man, I will give you that—save for the hand. Is that how you met him? Did he come to you for a cure or a charm?"

"Something like that."

Nellie switched her gaze back to Annie. "Aye, and you ha' the glow of a woman newly wed. I should know." She rested her hand on her swollen belly. She'd wed her Andrew last autumn, and the bairn inside was her first. "'Tis why I ha' come this day. My back has been hurting me something fierce. Ha' you a charm for that?"

Annie inspected her slowly. "I can give you a wee pouch to put beneath the ticking of your bed, but I doubt 'twill help. 'Tis the bairn's weight making you ache. You'll give birth within the week, unless I miss my guess."

"By heaven, I hope so." Nellie planted both hands in the small of her back and groaned. "How I wish your

79

mother were here for the birthing."

Annie wished it also. "You're fine and healthy. You'll do well."

Nellie stole another look at Tam. "Aye, and I do no' doubt you'll be in like straits to me before long."

Would she? The thought startled Annie even though she, who lived as best she might in accordance with the earth, knew it for the natural order of things.

Yet when she'd conceived this plan, she'd not dreamed of taking to her bed the man she brought home as husband. Indeed, she could not say how it had happened. Those intoxicating kisses of his, no doubt.

She let her gaze follow him around the yard, a bit dreamily. She'd not expected him to stay about the place this day. Her uncle had always fled, taking some of the dogs walking in the hills when the "troops of women," as he called them, arrived. Tam worked quietly stacking firewood at the side of the yard, only slightly hampered by his hand, and out where everyone could see him.

Annie felt glad. Suddenly she wanted all the world to know him for her man. *Hers*. And not just because of Ned Randleigh.

"There, now," Nellie said, "you canno' even look at him without smiling."

Annie hurried into the house to get Nellie her charm. When she returned, she found still more women crowding the yard.

Nellie gave her a penny for the charm and hurried off. A rough queue formed of women young and old, each with some urgent request.

"Have you anything for my aching fingers, lass?"

"Will you speak a charm over the head of my

bairn, here? He will no' stop greeting at night."

"My best hen has stopped laying and is pulling out her feathers. Have you a wee charm for that?"

They all went silent when Kirstie Brodach entered the yard, and every head turned as one. The lass—left alone on her croft save for her aging grandmother after the death of her father—came slowly, her head down, wrapped tight in her shawl.

Annie's heart plummeted; this boded ill indeed.

She left off explaining the uses of a salve to her latest customer and went to the gate at once. Kirstie's only real claim to beauty was that lent by youth; she could not be above sixteen, with soft, brown hair and a thin face that now bore telltale signs of weeping.

Annie's native compassion came to the fore; she seized Kirstie's hands. "Kirstie, lass, what is amiss?"

"My grandmother sent me." Kirstie did not look up and kept her voice so low Annie barely caught the words. "I am in a bad way."

Annie glanced around the yard. Everyone stared, including Tam, who had paused at his work. Inside the house, as she well knew, other women waited to have their tea leaves read.

"Come." She towed Kirstie around back, halfway down the track to the wee house where her uncle had set a bench beneath the trees, with only Ruff following. "Sit down."

Kirstie did, and Annie seized her hands. Cold as ice, they lay passive in hers.

"Kirstie, look at me. What has happened?"

The lass slowly raised her pale blue eyes. Her words came in a sudden rush. "Ye ken, mistress, how the factor has been after us all the winter long, saying I maun pay what we owe or he would be forced to toss us out."

"Aye," Annie agreed even as her stomach clenched.

"He returned two days ago, said his forbearance was at an end and I maun pay one way or another, else he would put my auld granny out into the cold."

Two days ago, when Randleigh had discovered she, Annie, had wed.

"So, so…" Kirstie began to weep. "I paid his price, but no' in coin. He has ruined me, mistress!"

Struggling to keep from betraying the extent of her dismay, Annie said, "You were intact, lass? He took your maidenhead?"

Kirstie nodded brokenly. "Not only that. He hurt me full well, mistress. 'Twas like a bull mating wi' a heifer, unco' rough. I—I started bleeding soon after, and ha' no' stopped since."

Rage joined the sickness in Annie's gut. "Is the bleeding bad?"

"Bad enough. And the pain—I think he tore me open, mistress. I wept and begged him to stop. He would no'."

"Och, Kirstie," Annie breathed. "Do you wish for me to examine you?"

Kirstie shook her head wildly. "No' wi' all these people about."

"We will go up to the loft. Come."

She towed the trembling girl into the house and up the ladder, telling Sonsie in passing, "Keep everyone away."

Kirstie wept throughout the examination, by the end of which Annie's hands shook with rage. *The beast.*

How could he use a tender young lass so? She attempted to thrust her anger aside and give Kirstie some reassurance.

"You will heal, lass. Did you tell your grandmother what happened?"

"Nay, but she heard. She heard it all."

"I will give you a potion wi' which to wash yoursel', and you must do it most carefully. Also, perhaps something to help you sleep."

Kirstie mopped at her pale cheeks. "Aye, but mistress, I came here for another sort o' potion—one to unseat a bairn if he has left one. Please!" She seized both of Annie's hands. "Tell me there is such a cure."

"There is." Though Annie had never given it out and her mother had warned most strongly against its use. *We are to do no harm, daughter. It is our first law.* Now, looking into the eyes of the distraught girl, she warned, "It does not always work, mind, and it may make you very ill."

"I do no' care. I swear to you, mistress, I will take my own life if I come up carrying his brat. Just as I will slay mysel' before ever accepting him again."

"List, lass. Do you want to come here and stay with me?"

"My grandmother will no' leave the place and is too ill to move, even if she would. That is why…" Kirstie took to weeping again. Annie pulled the lass into her arms in an attempt to lend comfort, even though rage still drummed in her ears.

But Kirstie soon drew away. "Tell me, Mistress Annie, you know many spells. Do you ha' any for keeping him away? Or—or for dealing wi' him? A fall from that horse o' his, mayhap…"

Gently, Annie said, "Kirstie, that would be black magic. You ken I will ha' no truck wi' it."

"But he deserves—"

"I ken fine what he deserves, and you speak the truth. Still, such punishment is no' ours to deal out. You maun let fate and the powers answer him."

"But they do not! What do I say if he comes to my door again?"

"Tell him he has had all he will from you. Kirstie, have you no neighbor or relation, no one who could come and stay wi' you?"

"No relations left alive, mistress, and the neighbors dare not cross him."

"Would it help if I sent Jockie to stay wi' you?"

"Him? The factor would take pleasure in venting his spleen on poor Jockie."

"The lad is stronger than he looks, and smarter."

But Kirstie shook her head.

"Come along, then. I will get those mixtures ready for you—and ask Jockie to at least see you home."

They climbed back down from the loft into a room now bursting with women who wished to consult the cards or the tea leaves. Annie whispered that Sonsie should try and stall them while she hurried to mix the cures for Kirstie.

The women chatted like magpies the whole time she worked and only fell silent when Tam entered the room and crossed to Annie's side. Into her ear he breathed, "What is the matter? You look unco' upset."

"I will tell you later. Find Jockie for me, will you please, and ask if he will see Kirstie, here, home. He is likely hiding in the byre."

"Aye." She felt his gaze touch her brow and chin.

"But, are you all right?"

"I am no' sure, husband. I am no' sure at all." For her faith bade her harbor no ill will. What then to do with this rage?

Chapter Thirteen

"And will you now see my future in the bottom o'
one of those cups?" Tam spoke lightly in an effort to
distract Annie from the trouble that visibly beset her,
bowing her like a weight on her shoulders.

A long and busy day it had been, but all the women
had at last departed back to their own hearthsides, most
carrying a bag of herbs and a charm or two. Tam had
been surprised to see they paid what they could,
becoming insistent about it if Annie tried to refuse.
Those who could not pay offered favors in return, but
none went away wanting.

His wife, he decided as he watched her clear away
the cups, was a gey kind woman with a generous heart.
She felt the travail of those who came to her as if it
were her own—he could see the truth of that reflected
in her eyes. A hard way to live, he acknowledged, but a
good one.

And he'd won the privilege of having such a
woman for his wife. Whatever could he have done to
deserve it?

She paused with two cups in her hands and gave
him a look. "Would you see your future, Tam
Sutherland? Most men do no' wish to know what lies
ahead for them. 'Tis the women who come worrying
over the fate of their bairns and their men."

"And can you see the future there, truly? Stars and

triangles, trees and animals—that is what I heard you saw this day. What do those tell you?"

"You would be surprised. All those things ha' meanings. I learned them at my mother's knee."

"Aye, so." He paused. "And are you ready to tell me what is troubling you?"

"I am not, yet. Let me read your leaves instead." She swung the kettle, still hot, over the fire, carefully washed out a cup, and measured the leaves. He watched how gracefully her hands moved as she worked and imagined them touching him later tonight. His throat went dry with anticipation.

"There, now." She set the cup on the table and gestured for him to sit. "You drink that and then turn the cup in your hand three times, thinking about what you wish to know. Turn it over in the saucer and let it drain; we shall see what it reveals."

"Sit with me." He caught her hand in his good one. "You ha' been on your feet all day."

She allowed him to pull her onto the bench beside him and sighed with what sounded like pleasure.

He gulped some tea and asked, "So why was Jockie needed to see that young lass home?"

Annie's face went so still it frightened Tam. Used to seeing her eyes snapping with life and her features reflecting every emotion, he did not know what to make of this.

Unexpectedly she said, "Tell me, Tam, what do you do wi' the hate?"

"Eh?" His gaze flew to hers.

"The sheer weight of hatred that falls black over the mind. I know you maun feel it. You've lost your parents, your good dog—and the use of your hand. But 'tis such an ugly emotion. I do no' want to harbor it."

Tam's thoughts flew, trying to ascertain whom this fair-hearted, loving woman might hate so. Ruefully, he said, "Sometimes the hate lends me strength and determination. That, along with my pride, kept me going after it happened. Told mysel' I would be cursed if I let what they did to me determine the balance o' my life."

"Aye, aye, there is strength in rage and anger, the sisters of hate. But such emotion steals from us, also, Tam. It robs the beauty from us, here." She touched her breast.

"I do not doubt you are right, but 'twould take a finer man than I to refrain from it." He drained his cup and turned it about awkwardly in his left hand before placing it face down to drain. "You ask what I do with it? I push it back, and trust it will serve me well when I need it. Now, you tell me, what has tapped your rage?"

"Ned Randleigh."

"The factor?" Tam's stomach muscles tightened. "What of him?"

"That lass who was here today, Kirstie—she told me he took his price from her, to let her stay in her wee bit o' cottage wi' her ailing grandmother."

"You mean—?"

"I do. And the man treated her most cruelly, rutting as a beast might. He hurt her right well. She says if she comes up carrying his bairn she will tak' her own life."

Tam started up. "Somewhat must be done about him."

Annie met his gaze. "Aye, and what?"

"A sharp knife in the dark would serve."

"Nay. The man is a devil, sure, but none should

blacken his or her soul with such a deed."

"I am certain someone might be found to take on the task."

"Who? You?" Annie's eyes, so dead a moment ago, flashed to life. "Nay." She seized his hand in both of hers. "Promise me you will no' go after him."

Nearly choking on his outrage, Tam said, "I will make you no such promise, not one I canno' be sure I will keep." He drew a breath. "Men like him—like them—need settling."

"Aye, but as I told Kirstie, 'tis for the fates and the powers to deal wi' them as they deserve." Her fingers caressed his. "I ha' been taught that everything we put out into the world comes back threefold. If we send out kindness, we receive still more kindness. Hate, that we will also receive. Randleigh will get what he has coming."

"Much good that does the lass he forced. And you ken full well 'tis what he did, even if she spoke agreement in her straits."

"I ken, Tam. But you maun trust."

"In justice?" He shook his head, and his lips twisted. "After what I ha' seen, and endured?"

"If no' in justice, then trust me." Her eyes beseeched him. "Can you do that? Here, let us see what the leaves say about your future." She freed her hands from his and turned the cup upright.

They both saw it at the same instant—the shape outlined in tiny leaves. A heart it was, nearly perfect save for the jagged line that divided it clear across.

"Love," Annie said, sounding nearly breathless.

"Aye." Even Tam could have figured that. Had he suffered so much and traveled so far only to find a place in this woman's warm, giving heart? Had fate directed him after all?

He pointed with his finger. "But what of that line there? What does it mean?"

Sounding reluctant she said, "Sundering. Parting. A division—"

"Nay." He set the cup down and turned to her. "Annie, I will no' have it." He kissed her, putting all his emotions into it—fear, protest, and raw desire. She opened to him like a flower to the sun, her need leaping to meet his.

He broke the kiss to tell her raggedly, "I do no' want to see the future after all. I do no' want to part from you."

"Husband." She caught his face between her hands and gazed into his eyes. "Husband, have hope. The line exists, aye. But you see the heart is still whole."

****

Annie lay abed in the darkened, quiet house and let her eyes range about the dim room. She could see the outlines of all her familiar furnishings and Sol's silhouette where he sat in front of the window. The fire popped as it died and logs shifted. Beside her, having just satisfied her full well, her husband slept.

She wished she might rest, also—curl into the warmth of his body and release the thoughts that dogged her. But it seemed she had no more chance of that than of flying to the moon. Instead, she wriggled closer to Tam and wondered about love. Did she love this man at her side, still little more than a stranger despite the intimacies they'd shared? Or did she merely want him? No question she felt desire whenever he came near her, and sometimes even when he did not.

He had only to look at her to set her alight.

Aye, and what a complication that made. She'd gone into this scheme with but one intention, keeping the wolf—Randleigh—from her door. She'd anticipated her "husband" would be nothing more than a hired man in all but name. She'd failed markedly to keep to that plan.

But did she love him? Ah, surely not. Fancying she loved him must be a mere product of her body's craving for his. Of course, that did not explain why she relished their quiet conversations, enjoyed watching the light flood his gray eyes when he smiled, or admired how his muscles rippled when he removed his shirt and came to their bed.

Well, and aye—perhaps the lust did account for that last.

And what of the heart in the cup? Pierced by a line or not, it denoted love. No arguing with the leaves, as her ma used to say.

But what was she to do with these feelings? He had come as a hireling, secured by a vow. That did not mean he would stay once all this trouble was over. Her heart protested that truth and the urge to keep hold of him made her snuggle closer still.

She threw a possessive arm over him and inhaled the beguiling scent of warm male, his alone. Bless the trouble, she thought, that brought him to me. And at last she closed her eyes.

Chapter Fourteen

"Speak slowly, Jockie. Take your time. Now what is amiss?"

Tam, hearing his wife's voice, left the house and entered the yard to find Annie engaged with the young man. Jockie, obviously greatly distressed, stood huddled before her, face working with the effort to speak and fingers tangled in his own white-blond hair. Even as Tam joined them he saw the lad yank at his locks in frustration.

Tam remembered Annie telling him he could communicate with Jockie if he chose, speak to and understand him. To Tam, the lad's speech sounded garbled at the best of times, and he was now clearly overset.

Jock made the mewling sound that frequently preceded his attempts at speech. His pale blue eyes moved to Tam where he stood and away again; his slightly misshapen face worked anew.

"Miss."

Tam blinked. A word!

Sonsie appeared from the house and Ruff came to press against Jockie's side. The lad, seeming to take comfort in the lurcher's presence, straightened his spine and produced another word.

"Afraid."

Annie's face brightened with comprehension. "Are

you speaking of Miss Kirstie?"

Jockie nodded violently and pulled his hair still harder.

"S-stayed."

"You saw her home as I asked and stayed the night? Jockie, is she all right? Did the factor, Master Randleigh, return?"

Another shake of the head. "Nay, but afraid."

"Miss Kirstie is very much afraid, aye. I ken. I tried to persuade her to come here and stay, but her grandmother will no' budge."

Jockie's eyes narrowed intently on Annie's face, and a spate of words ensued, none of them comprehensible to Tam.

Yet somehow Annie understood. She asked, "And has Miss Kirstie agreed to this?"

Jockie shrugged, spoke some more, and made a gesture toward Tam.

Annie nodded. "Well, so. And 'tis your choice, lad. You do no' need to ask my permission. Gather your things and go as you will."

Sonsie turned and slipped away back into the house. Annie stepped forward, drew the lad's fingers from his hair, and kissed his forehead.

"That for luck and blessing, Jockie. My love goes with you."

Tears filled the lad's eyes before he ducked his head and limped away toward the byre, Ruff at his heels.

Tam stepped up to Annie. "What was that about? Is he leaving?"

She looked at Tam. Tears stood in her eyes also, bright as jewels. "For a time. He says that now you are here to protect me, he need not stay. He wishes to go watch over Kirstie because he's seen how very frightened she is there alone."

Tam gazed away toward the byre in wonder. "How does Kirstie feel about that?"

"I gather Jock does not care. He will bed down in an outbuilding as he did last night."

"Does he understand what happened to Kirstie?"

"Och, aye—he is not stupid, whatever you suppose."

"I am not sure what to suppose about him," Tam admitted, "save you ha' raised him to be as compassionate as you are."

Annie smiled sadly. "I did no' raise him. He is but a few years younger than me. That is my mother's hand you see. If aught, he is more like my brother than my child."

She wrapped her arms about herself, and Tam urged, "Come inside for breakfast. You are cold."

She nodded, and they went in to find Sonsie laying the table, her expression grim.

"I do no' like it when things change," Sonsie declared, shooting Tam a dark look. "We were fine before he came."

"Nay," Annie objected, "we were no' fine. The truth is, Sonsie, we stood very nearly where poor Kirstie does now. In fact, I canno' keep from wondering—if I had no' found a way to keep Randleigh at bay, would he have approached that poor lass at all?"

Sonsie's expression eased, and she relented. "You canno' blame yoursel'. That man is a monster. Miss, you canno' protect everyone."

"I should ha' tried harder, as Jockie does even now.

94

Och, but I fear for the lad. If Randleigh returns while he is there, what will happen? Randleigh will take pleasure in flogging the lad or hurting him any way he may." She scrubbed at the tears trickling down her cheeks. "But I canno' hold Jock back, can I, nor keep him from doing as his heart bids."

"Here, sit down." Tam guided Annie to a bench at the table. "Sonsie, please get your mistress some tea."

"There is very little left after yesterday," Sonsie grumbled but hurried to obey.

Tam sat at Annie's side. "Something must be done about this man Randleigh—beyond the valiancy of that young lad."

"Perhaps I should write to the laird once more."

Sonsie sniffed. "He ignored your last letter."

"There is a chance it did no' reach him. I must try again—remind him of his friendship wi' my uncle, ask for mercy on behalf of the folk here."

"Or go to see him," Tam suggested.

Her eyes widened. "To Edinburgh?"

"Aye but write him first, and ask him to come see how things lie here."

"I can but try."

Sonsie placed a cup in front of Annie and went out into the yard.

Tam leaned toward his wife. "Tell me more about Jockie. You said your uncle rescued him from travelers. How long ago was that?"

"It must ha' been all of ten years ago, and he was about seven when we got him. That would make him seventeen now."

The lad looked younger, but as Tam acknowledged, that might be due to his crooked spine and hunched stature.

"His body ne'er grew right," Annie went on softly, "one side different from the other, as you see. And 'tis gey difficult for him to speak and be understood, mainly because his words trip over one another so fast. But there is naught wrong wi' his wits. My ma used to say, 'Only think how it must be, such a keen mind trapped in that body.' I wish you might ha' met her."

Tam stroked Annie's hair gently with his good hand. "I believe I can see much of what she was like, in you."

Annie met his gaze. "And what do you see?"

"She must ha' been unco' warm, wise…merciful. Wonderful." He leaned in and kissed her very softly.

She sighed, and her eyes filled again with ready tears. "'Tis no' easy trying to fill the place she left. She never seemed to second guess herself."

"And you do?"

"All the time. Like now—should I let Jockie go? What if he risks himself and is hurt terribly?"

"As you ha' said, 'tis his choice to make."

Once more she gazed into Tam's eyes. "It's not just Jockie; there's you. What would she think of me taking you to my bed?"

Tam's heart seized for an instant. "You are no' regretting that, are you?" Because if she turned him away, if she withdrew her warmth that had already penetrated clear through to his heart, he did not know how he would go on.

But she gave him a wobbly smile. "I feel many things for you, Tam Sutherland. No regret."

****

A week passed, seven nights of Tam Sutherland

96

sharing Annie's bed, each more beguiling than the last. Even through her worry and the endless work of her days, Annie found herself looking forward to nightfall, when Sonsie retreated to the loft and all the creatures settled, leaving her and Tam free to explore one another.

And explore Annie did. She now knew Tam Sutherland's body as well as her own, how he tasted everywhere, and how to win from him the most wondrous response. She believed a little magic surrounded them when they lay together in the big, warm bed.

Aye, she had learned much about her husband. He scarcely ever raised his voice or lost his temper; he had a wicked, dry sense of humor that sparked hers. And even when they were out in the yard going about their various, separate chores he could heat her blood with a single look.

Who would have thought? She, who'd believed herself impervious to the vulnerabilities that so often proved to be the downfall of other women—she now shivered just imagining this man's touch.

She strove to keep her mind on the matters at hand, wrote another letter to Laird Ardaugh, and sent it east on the mail coach. She walked to Kirstie's place twice out of worry for both the lass and Jockie, only to find them rubbing along well enough and not yet inflicted with the presence of the factor.

On the second visit, Tam insisted on walking with her, and they came home afterwards with his good hand holding hers. By the time she reached the farm, she could scarcely wait for Sonsie to go to bed.

Now on this sunny afternoon that felt more like

spring than winter, she worked in her herb garden while Tam mucked out the byre—usually one of Jockie's chores.

She was trying to decide whether the rue had survived the winter when she heard his voice at her ear. "Just look at this!"

She turned to him in surprise. Bits of straw threaded his hair, but his eyes gleamed with excitement. Before she could speak, he raised his bad hand before her face. Slowly and with great concentration, he closed the fingers one by one about the handle of the pitchfork held under his other arm.

"I could no' do that before. Aye, sure, the fingers are still crooked, but I can bend them, and there's some strength there, real strength."

Annie parted her lips in astonishment. "And the pain?"

"Far less than usual."

"'Tis wondrous, that!"

"It is all down to you." He caught her up in one arm and swung her off her feet. "'Tis your loving makes the difference—I am convinced of it."

"Well, I canno' say…"

"I can." He dove for her mouth and imparted a searing kiss. Annie's bones promptly melted.

Tam drew away far enough to say, "'Tis like a magic spell when I come to you. And there be magic in your fingers when you soothe my hand. I need more. And more. And more." He presented each request with a kiss, making Annie's head spin.

She laughed breathlessly. "I can certainly massage your hand throughout the day. In the morning—"

"Och, aye, in the morning. Afternoon as well, but I

am no' talking about the hand."

Annie blushed crimson. "We canno'! Sonsie…"

"What of Sonsie? Send her on an errand. Or better yet, come to the byre wi' me. I ha' just laid clean straw."

"Now?"

"Now." He kissed her again, and her toes curled. "I am that hungry for the taste of you, I just may perish. And are you no' sworn to keep all from harm?"

"I suppose I am, at that."

"Then I do no' see how you can refuse me."

Annie giggled with delight as he carried her to the byre, a trail of animals following. First came Ruff with a disapproving look on his narrow, scruffy face, and Ella close behind, with both goats, Fiona the doe, and a cat bringing up the rear.

Tam ignored them all. Leaving the byre door open, he carried Annie to a freshly cleared stall, where they caught the attention of Old Rake and the two resident cows.

He deposited her in the sweet-smelling straw even as Rake craned his neck to stare before Tam joined her in the makeshift bed.

"There, now, merciful lady. Begin wi' your healing."

She gazed into his eyes, her laughter suddenly flown. All at once her whole life seemed to focus in this moment, the warmth of Tam Sutherland, and the light in his silvery eyes. What did she see reflected there? Desire, aye. The humor she loved from him, and a measure of teasing. And more…

The word *love* still had not been spoken between them, not for all their physical joining. It would be

Laura Strickland

better if she did not come to love him, for in that direction lay fear and potential loss. In the past so many she loved—human and animal alike—had been taken from her. If she lost this man, she just might not survive.

Better, far better, to take what he offered—this warmth more precious than gold, the feeling of safety, and the laughter, the boundless waves of pleasure—and ask for nothing more.

Another of her mother's lessons came to mind: life gave what it gave. Best to live in the moment, and this moment was oh, so beautiful.

"Why do you look at me so?" Tam asked.

"How do I look at you?"

One side of his mouth curled. "As if I ha' grown an extra head."

"The one you have is more than sufficient. Have I ever told you, Tam Sutherland, that I find you unco' handsome?"

"Do you, now?"

"Och, aye. Even when I first saw you at the hiring fair, I thought so."

"Before you saw my ruined hand."

"Let me see that hand." She captured it in both hers, raised it to her lips, and kissed the palm. "Bless it."

"Again," he demanded.

"Eh?"

"Bless it again." His eyes danced. "And my lips, bless them also. My throat needs a blessing. Here, let me tak' off this shirt so you may bless my chest, and och, I am in sore need of blessing further down."

Annie laughed helplessly. "Are you, then?"

"As you shall soon see."

And for a goodly time, Annie forgot about the world outside the byre.

Chapter Fifteen

"Where is your wife?" The harsh words cut across the mist that filled the yard and halted Tam in his tracks even as a low growl issued from the throat of Ruff, who lay beside the house door. The lurcher got to his feet, hackles raised.

With good reason. Ned Randleigh sat his horse at the gate, glowering at Tam in the weak morning sun.

Tam shifted his grip on the shovel he carried in his good hand, and hatred poured through him, scorching hot. It surprised him how ugly that felt—shocked him to realize that in Annie's company he must have laid aside at least part of the dark emotions that had accompanied him since the terrible night his hand was crushed.

But now, so readily, the ugliness surged back.

"Not here," he said shortly. Annie had been summoned from their bed during the night to attend a lying-in.

"'Tis Nellie's first," she'd explained even as she dressed hastily. "'Twill reassure her if I am there."

Randleigh examined him from sharp eyes set far too close together in his narrow face. The man had the look of a rat, Tam thought. But nay, he should no' insult any rat with such a comparison.

"I can see that. I asked you where she's gone. I need a word with her."

As if Tam would tell him any such thing. "If you ha' business here, you can speak wi' me."

Randleigh sneered, but he swung down from his mount. Ruff promptly charged the gate, and Randleigh drew his riding crop.

"Call back that mongrel or I will beat him off."

Tam, the shovel still in his hand, rushed forward to stand at Ruff's side. Now only the iron gate separated them from the factor. "I would no' advise it."

Randleigh eyed Tam up and down. "Upstart. Do you think I don't know this 'marriage' of yours is a sham? I have been to Oban and spoken with the priest who performed the rite. Done with unseemly haste, it was."

"What's that to you?" Tam challenged.

"Eh?"

"You heard me. What's it to you how my wife and I wed, or that she's wed at all—save you had your own shameful plans for her. Aye, I ken fine what you ha' been getting up to in the district. Your kind use threats as a weapon and wear intimidation like a second skin."

"My kind? What do you know of it—a ruffian from nowhere?" Randleigh pronounced it deliberately. "A nothing. She would have done better with me."

Tam felt the impact of those words like hurled stones. Were they true? Annie with all her talents, the wisdom in her head, her book learning, and the magic that trailed from her like scent—could he possibly be worthy of her? Nay, for in truth she had taken him only because no one else remained at the fair once she found the courage to make her request.

Randleigh smiled slightly as if he knew he'd scored a hit. He put his hand to the gate, and Tam raised the shovel to bar his way. Ruff pressed against Tam's side and raised the intensity of his growl; Tam could feel the dog trembling.

"Nay," he said. "You will no' set foot on this place."

Randleigh reared indignantly. "Tell your wife I am addressing all landholders; the laird has increased his requests for rent, effective the quarter that ends the last day of this month."

"Demands, you mean."

"Eh?"

"Demands, no' requests." Tam had lived all this before and knew how it went. The rents increased until the tenants could no longer pay and the factor might cite the law in order to throw them off the land.

"Call it what you will. The laird has increased the rent by one tenth. Since your wife is his tenant, make sure she knows."

Tam thought furiously. "That gives us less than a fortnight to come up wi' the increase."

Randleigh lifted a brow. "I may be able to arrange for more time—but I will negotiate only with your wife, mind. As I say, you are not the tenant."

Nearly speechless with anger, Tam croaked out, "I will be damned."

"No doubt. A curious thing—I supposed Mistress MacCallum so particular with her favors, until I heard the rumor she'd taken you to her bed."

Rage burned so hot behind Tam's eyes it turned his vision white.

"Get back on your horse," he said, sounding very like Ruff, "and ride off."

Randleigh sniffed but turned away. Ready to

remount, he looked back at Tam. "Oh, the priest at Oban—what was his name?"

"Father Alban."

"That is it, yes. He states you and Mistress MacCallum had been acquainted for a time, had in fact met when she visited him previously, as you had been staying with him."

Tam felt a flash of surprise at the priest's defense. "So?"

"So a bit odd that, in such circumstances, you did not post any banns."

"I was no' from that parish," Tam said steadily. "That is why."

Randleigh swung up onto his horse. "Also odd that several merchants of Oban cite a rumor that a woman looking very like Mistress MacCallum went to the hiring fair and spoke out, requesting a husband rather than a hired hand. Apparently, you responded."

"'Twas a joke, that. The two of us were playing wi' each other." Tam added deliberately, "As lovers do."

"Is that so?"

"It is."

Randleigh drew his horse up with a cruel hand. "Make sure you acquaint your wife with all I have said, Sutherland. With all of it, mind." And the factor rode off, scattering mist.

****

"A fine wee lad for all your travail," Annie pronounced and stood back in satisfaction to regard the little family. Nellie sat upright in the bed, flushed with victory and exhaustion, the new bairn in her arms. Her husband, Angus, leaned over them both, looking overjoyed.

105

Annie dried her hands on a cloth. "You would ha' done fine without me, Nell. No need to call me next time."

"I like having you here—it makes me feel safe," Nellie confessed. "Bless the bairn before you go?"

"If you wish." Annie whispered the ancient words, made signs to the four directions and laid her fingers on the bairn's forehead.

"There, now," Nell said in satisfaction. "He will be safe from all harm."

If only it were so easy, Annie thought.

Someone rapped at the door of the croft house. Annie left the new family and hurried away in response, only to find Tam, looking tall and handsome but with trouble in his clear, gray eyes.

"Tam! Why are you here? Is something amiss back on the farm?"

"I came to walk you home."

"Fine, that. I am just about finished. Let me gather my things."

She hurried back inside, wondering. She had begun to learn her husband's moods, and despite his calm words sensed something had upset him. But she bade the new family good bye and joined Tam with a smile.

"Never say you missed me so?" she asked as he took her basket, and she linked her arm through his.

He failed to return the quip, and his expression remained guarded. "Randleigh stopped by not long since."

Annie's high spirits drained away like ale from a cracked cask. "He did? What did he want?"

Tam steered her down the track and a short distance along the brae before he answered. "He said he has orders from the laird to increase rents at the end of this month."

"Och, nay! But folk canno' stand to pay any more. There are those in the district who already canno' pay what they owe. I feel guilty every time they give me a penny for a cure or a charm."

Tam eyed her. "And what of us? Can we stand an increase?" He shrugged his shoulders uneasily. "I ken fine I am of no use to you, no' bringing in a wage or aught."

Annie rounded on him. "You are of great use to me. What would I do wi' out you now that Jockie is gone to help Kirstie?"

He returned her look, something unreadable in his eyes. "Just another Jockie to you, am I?"

"Nay—"

"I should no' be surprised. Did you no' go to the fair looking for naught more than a hand by another name?"

Annie stopped walking and faced him. Behind his head the late morning sky shone gray with cloud—as gray as his eyes—streaked with bars of brightness from the struggling sun.

What to say to the man? That aye, she had gone to the fair with the intention of hiring a husband, very little different from taking on a hand. That she had never intended to take him to her bed, never imagined involving her heart. That the thought of him walking away now made her so breathless she feared she might perish.

Her feelings had changed. Did he not know that? Must she speak the word—love—outright?

Och, and how could she? It gave him a power over

her she'd never lent anyone—the ability to wound, to leave her heart far more maimed than ever his hand had been.

She drew breath. "Surely you know you are much more than that to me now."

"Do I?" He freed himself from her clinging fingers and waved the basket wildly. "You who might have chosen any man—wealthy, educated—to be landed wi' the worst leavings o' the hiring fair."

"Fate blessed me that day."

"How? I possess no means to help you, save my presence and my name. Any man could ha' kept the threat of Randleigh from your bed."

Did he truly believe that? Could he not feel the truth when she touched him, ran her fingers over his strong shoulders, down the plane of his belly and lower still? Did he not know she delighted in his smile, loved to watch the breeze ruffle his thick brown hair? Enjoyed listening to him whistle as he worked about the yard?

His presence had become far more than presence— her need and desire.

"Tam," she began.

But he interrupted her. "Randleigh went to see Father Alban."

Her eyes went wide. "Did he!" Ah, and what had he discovered there? Were they undone? Did she risk losing Tam after all?

"The priest lied for us, said I had been staying wi' him and so we became acquainted. I told Randleigh the scene at the fair was just us playing wi' one another— as lovers do—implying we always intended to wed."

As lovers do. "And did he believe you?"

Tam shrugged. "Who can tell? On the whole, I think not."

Annie drew another breath. "Well, we are wed, for all that, so he canno' take you from me." She caught his gaze. "Tam, tell me naught can take you from me."

Tam turned away. "I ha' given you my word, have I no'? And my word means something. Now, come, let us haste home."

Chapter Sixteen

"Mistress Annie, Mistress Annie! You maun come!"

The cry at the door had Ruff on his feet and Annie sitting upright in the bed, her heart pounding. Darkness still filled the house, the embers of the fire a mere glow in the hearth. A dream? For an instant, she almost thought so.

But nay, for all the animals now stirred; both dogs had their heads up, and Sol rustled his wings in agitation. And Annie's husband, who slept beside her? Last night had been the first in many they had not made love. Instead, he had turned away from her in the big bed. She needed to get to the bottom of that—

Pounding resumed at the front door. No dream, then. She stirred and started to rise, but Tam, not asleep after all, caught her arm.

"I will go."

He arose and struggled into his trousers; she could see him but dimly. Failing to follow his implied directions, she swiftly arose and followed him, pausing at his shoulder when he swung wide the door.

Kirstie, breathless and weeping, tumbled in and reached for Annie with desperate hands.

"Mistress, och, 'tis so terrible, too terrible! He came back—he returned this night, bent on…on…"

"Randleigh?"

The lass nodded, so winded and choked by tears she could barely speak.

Annie's heart fell violently, but she said, "Take a moment, Kirstie. Here, sit."

Tam, silent, struck a light. By its radiance Annie could see Kirstie's frantic expression and tense fingers clutching at one another.

"You maun come," she said again when she could speak. "He is hurt awful bad."

"Who? Randlcigh?"

"Na, na!" Kirstie shook her head. "Jockie. He tried to get between the factor and me. Och, he was so brave!"

Annie's stomach turned. "What happened?"

"Randleigh beat him with that crop he carries—you ken the one." Kirstie held out her hands so they could see her wrists, now crisscrossed with welts. "I tried to stop him."

Tam cursed. Annie clasped the lass's hands. "And did Randleigh then leave? List to me, lass—he did no' violate you again?"

"Nay." Kirstie shook her head. "But he would ha' done, if Jockie were no' there. Och, Jockie is such a hero! But sore hurt…"

"How bad is it?"

"Bad. You maun come and help him."

Annie looked at Tam helplessly.

"You will no' go alone," he said in a grim voice. "I am coming along wi' you."

"But we canno' leave Sonsie here alone," Annie began.

The girl, having come down from the loft and heard all, spoke up. "Yon beast will no' want to try me—no' with this face." She gestured to her harelip. "You go to Jockie, miss, and hurry."

"Aye. Let me gather some supplies."

Sonsie tried to comfort Kirstie while Annie hastily collected what she needed, her hands shaking almost too badly to serve. Tam, suddenly at her side, took the supplies from her, his one good hand steadier than her two.

"Here, let me."

"This is all my fault," she lamented in a voice pitched for his ears alone. "I never should ha' let him go there."

"Would it ha' been better to let Randleigh have his way wi' that lass again?"

"Och, nay."

"Besides, you said yoursel', Jockie is grown. You could no' hold him."

"But Ned Randleigh has always hated him, treated him like naught but an animal. I should ha' known he would be terrible harsh—even more so than usual—if Jockie got in his way."

Tam caught her shoulders between his hands and turned her toward him. Looking into her eyes, he said, "Annie, you maun let Jockie be a man. 'Tis for him to choose."

"Aye, right. You are right. I think I ha' what I need. Let us haste."

She went to Sonsie. "Bar the door behind us, mind. And do no' open it to anyone."

****

The moon kept pace with them as they went over the brae, Kirstie leading the way at a hectic pace. Ground mist swirled about Tam's knees, and he kept one eye on his wife—whom he'd never seen so distraught—and the other cocked for signs of Randleigh on his big, black horse.

Yet the world seemed unnaturally quiet, like something in a dream.

Kirstie's croft proved a wee bit of a place, barren even in the dark. The girl ran on ahead, saying over her shoulder, "I had to leave the door unbarred. Granny canno' get up from her bed to let me in, and Jockie—" Her throat worked, and she desisted.

"All right, so. We are here now," Annie said breathlessly.

Inside, poverty showed everywhere. A single lamp burned, illuminating the poor furnishings and the bed in the corner where the old grandmother lay. Sweeping the room with his eyes, Tam focused on a figure lying beside the hearth, even as Kirstie hurried forward.

"Jockie! Jockie, lad, can you hear me?"

Clearly senseless, Jockie made no response. Both women hunkered down, one on either side of him, and Tam stationed himself at the door, silently vowing no one else should enter.

He watched as Annie touched the lad with gentle hands. "Senseless," she confirmed. "Likely a mercy. By all that is holy!"

Tam narrowed his gaze. Even in the poor light he could see the extent of Jockie's injuries. In fact, apart from his familiar clothing, Tam might not have recognized the lad; his features could barely be discerned for blood. Annie's hands faltered before reaching out with now-familiar compassion. Tam could almost feel her thinking. Where to touch? How best to help?

"What is it? Wha' is happening?" the old woman cried piteously from the bed.

"Hush, Granny. Mistress Annie, I told you it was bad. Is he dead?"

"Dead? Nay, lass—still breathing. Bring me some water. Let us sponge this blood away and see how dire it is."

Kirstie hurried to obey, and Annie opened her parcel, murmuring to Jockie all the while.

"There, now, lad—I hear you ha' been a hero. Did I no' always say you had it in you? Can you open your eyes for me?"

"Let him lie." Even from where he stood, Tam could see Randleigh must have gone mad with rage when he attacked the lad. Blood covered not only Jockie's face but his hands, which he no doubt had raised in an effort to defend himself. His shirt lay in shreds.

"Here." Kirstie plopped down a basin, the water slopping over. "Och, miss, please help him. I could no' bear it if he perished on my account."

Annie said nothing but began to sponge away the blood slowly and carefully, revealing the horrific wounds beneath. Forgetting his post, Tam stepped forward to see.

He had never before beheld Jockie at rest. Indeed, with his usual facial contortions eased, he appeared almost ordinary—save for the new, livid wounds. They marked his wide forehead, bisected his nose, and scored his cheeks. Even his eyes had collected pools of blood.

Kirstie began to weep again. "He was so brave. You should ha' seen him, miss. He put himself in harm's way for me."

"Aye," Annie murmured, "and I could no' be more proud of him, not if he were my own brother. Bring another wee bowl of water, Kirstie, so we can stir in these herbs. And let us get this shirt off him."

"Let me help." Tam hunkered down beside Annie and lifted the lad so Kirstie could peel away the bloodied shirt. When she finished, he said, "Get a rug to put beneath his head."

The lass leaped to respond.

"Who are you?" the grandmother asked Tam querulously from the bed. "Are you the man who hurt my granddaughter?"

"Nay, old mother, not I," Tam responded. He ran his gaze over Jockie, and his stomach turned. Few would use an animal so. Hate rose within him in a violent wave. Randleigh needed answering for this.

"Will he be all right?" Still weeping, Kirstie sank to her knees at Jockie's side.

"I pray so. I canno' say." Tam had never seen his wife's expression so grim. "Poor lad."

Poor, indeed—Jockie had never been a beauty; now he might bear scars, as well.

"Why does he no' wake?"

Annie felt carefully around the lad's skull. "I think he hit his head when he went down. Did he fall hard?"

"Yon beast of a man beat him down. He fought to stand but had no weapon."

"Aye, well," Tam breathed, "we will correct that lack."

Kirstie looked at Tam wonderingly but went on, "Randleigh kept striking him even after he fell. I screamed and screamed at him."

"Screamed," the grandmother confirmed spectrally

from the bed.

"But what shall I do?" Kirstie continued to weep. "I still ha' no money to pay the rent, and Master Randleigh says there is to be an increase."

"Do no' fret over that now. Help me wash these wounds and get them bound. Gently, mind."

Tam returned to the door, opened it, and peeked outside. Dawn grayed the sky, lending the barren yard a bleak, ghostly air. No sign of Randleigh—barely a sign of anything save a few scrawny hens.

A groan pulled him back inside. Jockie had begun to come around. The lad's eyes flicked open, and Annie bent over him.

"Jockie, can you see me, lad?"

"Aye."

"Do you ken what's happened to you?"

"Aye," Jockie grunted again. "Randleigh." He followed the name with a choice epithet that made Tam smile reluctantly. The lad had the factor's measure, and no mistake.

"A hero you are, a hero!" Kirstie told Jockie forcefully, and he gazed at her through rapidly-swelling eyelids, looking dazed.

"Kirstie, have you any extra blankets? We will make a bed for him right here beside the fire. I do no' think we can get him home just yet."

Kirstie sprang up. "Nay, but I want him to stay. I will go get him my bedding." More softly still, she repeated, "I want him to stay."

Chapter Seventeen

Still another crofter squeezed through the gate into Annie's yard, and she wondered how many more might arrive. They had been showing up all morning, some walking far to join this gathering.

Just why it should take place in her yard, Annie could not say, save for the fact that in the past, if unable to go to the laird, these folk would have instinctively turned to her uncle. And the women so often came to her, Annie, for help and advice.

Many women now held places in the crowd, some with their men and a few alone. Word of what had befallen Jockie had spread quickly, as had news of the increase in rents. Concern now marked the faces of those gathered, along with open fear.

Three days had passed, and Jockie's condition had improved; he now moved about under his own power, though Annie could only imagine his discomfort. He refused to talk about Randleigh's attack, even when Annie got him alone.

And Kirstie, adamant, refused to let him leave her place, though Annie would have preferred bringing him home to heal, if only for her own peace of mind, for she wanted to make sure his wounds healed clean. And she kept thinking about the chances of Randleigh returning to harass Kirstie, and Jockie trying to stand in her defense again.

Now, if she could judge from the number of people crowding her yard, feeling in the district seemed to have reached a high pitch.

Annie, standing by her house door with Tam at her side, couldn't be sure whether they had come because of Jockie or the rent increase, but she heard the name "Randleigh" spoken like a curse on all sides.

Tam glanced at her questioningly, and she gave him a half shrug. Their relationship had regained a measure of ease since they'd gone to Kirstie's together in the night, but whatever troubled him rode him still; they had made love only once, and he had turned from her quickly, right after.

Annie's heart hurt just thinking of it. She'd tried to speak to him, but the words stopped in her throat when she saw the look in his eyes.

Yet he had been there every time she needed him, insisting on accompanying her when she walked to Kirstie's, doing a thousand small chores around the farm. And he stood firm beside her now.

That knowledge gave her courage to lift her chin and call out, "Neighbors and friends, I expect you are all gathered here because of what our laird's factor, Ned Randleigh, has done to Jockie MacCallum."

"We be here about these increases to t' rent!" called a male voice from the rear of the crowd. "What's to be done about it?"

Those gathered muttered vociferously. Maggie Abernathy stepped forward. "I am here about the rents, aye. But I am also here because o' what is happening to the women of this district. Yon factor, Randleigh, thinks he can come to an unmarried woman and demand what he wants. And I ha' three daughters."

Women's voices rose all around in support of her words.

"Aye, so," Annie said when the furor died down. Had she not been forced to take a husband for that very reason? She stole a look at Tam. Not that she regretted it…

An older man stepped forward. "What's to be done? Were your good uncle still here, lass, he would ha' spoken to the laird on our behalf."

"Where is the laird?" asked another woman. "Why has he turned his back on us?"

A new ripple spread through those gathered. When Annie could make herself heard, she said, "I have written to the laird telling him how his factor misuses us and appealing to him for intervention."

"Aye, and has the high-and-mighty Laird Ardaugh answered ye, lass? Has he come home to see what hardships visit his clan folk?"

"Nay," Annie had to admit.

"Nay! And will no', I'll be bound!"

"I ha' heard," someone else put forth tentatively, "the laird is ill and 'tis sore difficult for him to travel in his age."

"Sore difficult?" A woman fairly spat. "I will tell you what is sore difficult—raising seven weans on what little we ha' left after the laird gets his share. And now he would steal even more from my bairns' mouths."

"'Tis too easy for the laird to ignore a letter," said another man. "Someone needs to go and see him, tell him just what 'tis like for us under the heel of his factor. Life was better when the laird lived here on the land."

"Aye, miss!" Several voices took it up. "You maun

journey to see him on our behalf."

"Me?" Annie's head spun. She could barely imagine traveling as far as Edinburgh.

"Aye, so!" The words became a clamor.

"Your uncle would ha' gone."

True, Dennis MacCallum had been to Edinburgh, Stirling, Glasgow, Dundee—even, once, to London.

"I am not my uncle," she answered, "and have responsibilities here." What might happen to Jockie and Sonsie if Annie went? What if she returned only to find Tam gone?

A man suggested, "Your new husband can look after things here whilst you are away."

Annie shook her head. "Let me think on it. In the meantime, I suggest we band together in vigilance and seek to protect those among us who are women living alone."

"And get what Jockie got?" asked a man. "I ha' a family of my own to look after. How am I to do that if I take a thrashing from the factor?"

"Better," said another man darkly, "to wait along one of the roadways, a lot of us together, and take care o' the factor when he rides by."

A low rumble started among those gathered and arose fitfully.

Annie raised her hands. "I canno' speak to such a course of action. Punishment could come swift and hard…"

"Aye, but where is the factor's punishment for thrashing young Jockie or thinking he can tak' what he wants from our daughters?" cried still another woman. "Where the justice?"

"There is no justice for such as us," said an older

man, and the grumbling swelled again.

Beside Annie, Tam shifted on the balls of his feet. Like her, did he feel the mood shifting to something very nearly out of control? For Annie suspected if the factor rode into her yard now—not that he could fit—he might just be beaten to death by this crowd.

She drew a breath. How to calm them and answer their fears—to help them? For, as so often, she felt she stood in her uncle's—her mother's—place.

Clearly she said, "Our situation, aye, is dire. But I would ask you to keep hope. So far, Laird Ardaugh has cleared very few from their homes, unlike in other places. That shows he does feel for us. An attack on his factor, no matter how well-deserved, might alter the laird's attitude for the worse and solve nothing. I canno' argue for violence in answer to violence."

She felt Tam quiver at that and wondered at his response. Tam Sutherland so seldom revealed his emotions. When he did, it seemed a precious gift—but one denied to her now.

Those gathered in the yard took exception to her opinion.

"The factor needs a thrashing like he dealt your lad."

"We canno' sit still beneath his tyranny!"

The wave of anger rose again, and once more Tam shifted. At last Annie called, "I will think on going to speak wi' the laird. Until then, as I say, be vigilant on behalf of one another. Band together o' the nights, if you can. But do naught that will cost you dear."

Would they accept her direction? Anne had no real authority beyond what lingered in her uncle's wake, and many a hothead populated the crowd. They muttered and argued among themselves before they at last began to trickle away by ones and twos, as they had come. Many of the women came to Annie before they left, to ask favors—charms or wee spells for protection, mostly.

Many began with the words, "I canno' pay, but…"

Annie answered their needs anyway, taking freely from her stores, urging watchfulness and caution. By the time the last of them left and the yard stood empty, she felt drained.

"Come, mistress," Sonsie urged then. "Sit and drink some tea."

"Is there any left?" Annie went inside and carefully stowed away the few pennies she'd been given.

"I ha' scraped some together for you."

"Thank you, Sonsie, dear."

Annie sat at the table and put her head in her hands. She felt someone touch her back in comfort. Tam? She so longed to turn to him, take refuge from this storm in his arms. But nay, it was Sonsie, setting the cup before her.

"What am I to do?" she wondered aloud. "I ha' no' the ability to direct those folks. I fear I am a poor substitute for Ma and Uncle Dennis, even though I ha' tried." To her horror, tears flooded her eyes and stopped her throat.

Tears solve nothing, her mother used to say. But she knew all too well she lacked her mother's strength.

She lifted her gaze to Tam, who stood just inside the door watching her. If only she might be sure he was with her completely, she could face anything.

Silently, he turned his back and let himself out into the yard.

Chapter Eighteen

Tam entered the house quietly, his step careful. Outside, the evening drew down, a red sunset bleeding through angry gray clouds. A poor omen for the morning to come, and an apt reflection of the storm in his heart.

At the time of his father's death, he'd believed he could feel no greater pain. Then he'd lost his mother, and the gulf in his heart grew to desperate proportions.

With her warmth and caring, with her touch both on his ruined hand and his damaged soul, Annie had begun bringing him back from that dark and terrible place. Yet tomorrow morning she would go from him at the demand of that same compassion he so admired in her, reopening the gulf in Tam's soul.

He'd begged her to let him journey to Edinburgh at her side. The thought of her going without him shook him deeply, both because he feared for her safety on such a long journey and because the time apart from her defied imagining.

He'd tried to tell her that, but words had failed him. She wanted him here looking after Sonsie and the animals, and Kirstie's household, as well. She intended, instead, to travel with an older man called Rory MacBain, who had always found favor with the laird. Now, shutting the door on that angry sunset, Tam knew he had but one night to convince her otherwise.

He looked up and found her dark eyes on him, deep and measuring. Her bag, all packed, stood by the wall; they had returned not long since from Kirstie's and yet another attempt to convince that lass's old grandmother to come stay here for the duration.

The old woman, though, had not been swayed, declaring, "I was born here and will die here!"

Tam, standing by and watching it all, thought to himself, aye—when yon factor tosses you out, bed and all.

Before he and Annie left Kirstie's, Tam had approached Jockie, now on his feet if still moving as if he hurt, and slipped him a pocket knife. Small comfort against the factor's whip, but at least the lad would not go unarmed.

"Come and eat," Annie told him now. "Sonsie has made a fine supper for us."

Tam nodded, though he feared he might choke if he tried to swallow food. He took his seat at the table, and Ella crowded close to his legs; the wee dog, just like Ruff, sensed the discord. Even Sol ruffled his feathers uneasily.

"Best to eat and then an early night, miss," Sonsie urged. "You leave at dawn."

An early night. Desire clawed at Tam's belly, and he looked at his wife again. They'd made love only once in the last week, when his need overcame his restraint. Would she accept him this night? Might he show her thus his feelings, for which he had no words?

Annie often chattered throughout their meals, teased Sonsie gently, and spoke to the animals. This evening she remained very nearly silent. Sonsie, who attempted a limping conversation, at last gave it up and rose to gather the dishes.

When Annie made as if to rise also, the girl told her, "Nay, you stay there at your ease."

Annie turned at last to Tam. "I must confess I feel ill prepared for this journey. My mother would ha' taken it in stride, girded herself up, and gone off into the breech like a warrior." She wrinkled her brow. "It becomes abundantly clear I am no' my mother, no matter how I try."

He reached both hands across the table. "You are stronger than you think." Strong enough, if she but knew it, to lend him her will, to light his life he'd believed would be forever dark.

She took his bad hand in both of hers and began massaging it in that wondrous way she had, her very touch a balm.

"You promise to check on Jockie whilst I am gone?"

"Aye."

She hesitated, and her dark gaze searched his. She lowered her voice to ask, "And will you miss me, Tam Sutherland?"

"You know I will." He used her hands to draw her close across the table, and claimed her lips gently. Fire flared in his heart and lower down, as well. How could he let her go?

Her lips responded to him avidly, as if she'd been starving for him. How might that be, when he'd come to her by a chance of fate? But surely he did not mistake the need that flooded upon him.

When the kiss broke she whispered, "Tam…"

He glanced at Sonsie, who busied herself beside the hearth. Would the lass never finish her tasks and go

125

to her bed? An early night, she'd said—by heaven, it could not come early enough.

****

At last all the chores were done, dishes and pots lined up on the cupboard, fire banked, and animals let out for the night. Sonsie had disappeared up the ladder to the loft. Annie and her husband were alone.

Annie drew a breath. She doubted she mistook Tam's intentions this night. True she—who usually found others wondrously easy to read—had difficulty divining his emotions much of the time. He kept that handsome face shuttered, the gray eyes well-guarded as if to hide the pain that lurked inside. But Annie had tasted that pain, and the desire he hid equally well.

She longed for many things as she stood watching Sonsie disappear up the ladder—for a reprieve from this journey that loomed over her, for the courage to tell this man how she truly felt about him. To take him to her bed and love him so he might never doubt her again.

By all that was holy, she would have one of the three—two, if she might scrape up the courage.

Even as she wondered how to find it, Tam blew out the lamp and approached her in the light shed by the banked fire. Its radiance washed over him and showed her the intent look in his eyes as he drew her close and threaded his fingers through her hair.

"Annie."

Her name on his lips, only that, yet it affected her deeply. What did he feel at this moment? She longed to know. A man of few words, Tam Sutherland—she'd learned that much. But now he gazed into her eyes and said, "I wish you did no' have to go."

"And I."

"It will no' be the same wi' you gone."

Annie's heart trembled and then accelerated with joy. But what of the distance that had lately existed between them? Cursed if she would remind him of that now.

Instead she leaned in and kissed him. Their lips, mouths, tongues met and fused; heat spread all the way to Annie's toes.

Please, she thought at him because she would not surrender his mouth to speak.

In answer, he reached for the laces on her bodice, his right hand fumbling only slightly over the task. She gloried as each garment fell away from her and hit the floor, all while their mouths remained melded. At last, naked, she pressed against him, trembling with need.

You. Following the impetus of desire, she pulled at his shirt, drew it from him with lingering caresses on his neck and shoulders. Heaven lay in the way it felt when her breasts met the soft hair on his chest; the heat and weight of him lower down rendered her breathless. When she reached for the laces on his trousers, he swept her up off her feet and carried her to the bed.

Heaven deepened like the coming night as he shed his clothes and they moved together, naked and entangled, between the blankets, the stillness broken only by the pop of the fire as it settled. If Annie had the power to seize time, draw out these moments and make them last forever, she would do so and spend eternity in this man's arms.

For she adored the way he tasted, the feel of his warm skin beneath her fingers, and his tangy scent. She loved the way he caressed the inside of her mouth with his tongue and the way his lean hips fit so perfectly between her thighs. She loved the feel of his wavy hair caught between her hands when he abandoned her mouth at last to seek out her breasts one after the other, his mouth hot and wet, claiming and connecting her to him—connecting him to her soul.

And bless him, he did not stop at her breasts. Precisely as if he heard the desire screaming through her blood, he continued to caress her with that searing mouth—the soft skin of her stomach, one hip, her upper thigh, down one leg and up the other as if he had missed every inch of her and needed to taste it again. All the while she could feel the searing weight of him pressed against calf and knee, yet he refused to let her capture him between yearning hands and at last made her forget even that desire, when his questing mouth hovered between her thighs.

Then Annie forgot all words—forgot to breathe—as she willingly opened herself to him, body and spirit all in one—denying him nothing, to the last drop of her blood.

She knew in that moment what she felt for Tam Sutherland went far beyond the physical, to spiritual binding.

But oh, the physical part of it! For his mouth became part of her, and the chord he struck, trembling, vibrated through her, on and on. Even then his mouth continued to play her, tasting what she yielded up so generously and coaxing a still deeper response.

When she lay open, seared as if cast on a far shore, he worked his way back up her body, leaving kisses as he came. Only when he reached her ear did he whisper, "Does that tell you how I feel for you, Annie? Does it? I ha' no words, but…"

Did it? True enough, there were no words for such a joining. She didn't attempt to find them. Instead, she caught his face between her hands and kissed him deeply before working her way down his body in turn.

Throat hot and pulsating, chest abrading her lips with that enticing pattern of hair, taut belly that flexed beneath her tongue, and then her goal at last, pulsating also and searing her lips.

He moaned, the sound torn from him, and trembled as her mouth accepted him. But before she could begin to glory in his intoxicating flavor he gasped, flipped her beneath him and laid claim to her mouth even as he plunged into the place that lay so perfectly readied for him.

Light flashed once more behind Annie's eyes, and her euphoria became complete.

Breath ragged, they lay while he remained inside her and the spell woven over time held. Tears flooded Annie's eyes. Now—she should tell him how she loved him. But could he not tell?

Very slowly, as if with reluctance, he withdrew from her. The spell broke and reality crashed in.

"Annie, do no' go to Edinburgh."

"I must. I do no' want to, but I must." She clung to him, and the tears spilled over. "I canno' let everyone down. They come to me in my uncle's stead, in my mother's. I feel if I do no' measure up I will be letting him, and her, down as well."

Tam said nothing, and she confided, "At the same time I dread facing the laird and trying to persuade him. I was but a girl last I saw him. He may not even remember me."

Tam stirred. "Let me go wi' you. The journey is

long; I would be at your side."

What a comfort that would be! The strength of him beside her, the bliss of not having to part... But she shook her head.

"I am that afraid of leaving Sonsie and the animals here on their own. Who will watch over the place, with Jockie still at Kirstie's? Who will watch over Jockie, for all that? I trust you, Tam, to look after all I hold dear."

Again he did not speak, but she felt his emotions rise like a wave. As if to comfort him, she whispered, "Hold my place for me, Tam, till I return."

Chapter Nineteen

Tam glanced for the third or fourth time down the lane that led away from Annie's gate—as if he thought he would see her returning so soon. She had left just yesterday morning, traveling with Rory MacBain, who seemed a sturdy sort and had a cart with a good team. The journey would take many days. Unless something happened to make them turn back, he would not see her yet.

That did not keep him from longing.

Their parting yesterday had gone hard with him. After the intensity of their joining the night before—the sheer blistering intimacy of it—he felt seared and full of chagrin, despising himself for failing to tell her what he truly felt. But in the light of morning, the flurry of leaving, with Sonsie and MacBain present, he had no second chance.

Even though she'd looked so beautiful it made his heart hurt, clad all in her green gown and cloak as he'd first seen her, with Sol's feather bobbing in her hat and her black eyes snapping.

Wee Crow, her uncle had called her, and it fit. Watching her so, all decked out and spurred by intent, made him love her all the more, even as he experienced his unworthiness. Who was he to deserve such a woman?

But when the furor died down, once they'd parted

with just a lingering touch of hands, he discovered she'd taken all the joy with her, the life—the magic from this place. He'd not realized till then how he'd been living on the strength of that magic, but he had.

Now he felt like a petulant child, thoughts he neither wanted nor needed running through his mind. To be sure, Annie lived to serve others: Sonsie and Jockie, all her beloved creatures, her neighbors, and those who came to her for help. But what of him? Did she not consider him at all in her reckoning, how it would feel for him living without her, even if only for the span of a few days, how he needed her?

Nay, fool, for you ha' no' told her. You ha' failed to dredge up the words from your heart and present them to her ears.

He should have done just that, should have told her last night after he'd tasted her so deeply it felt as if part of her spirit had mingled with his, when she lay shedding tears over the task ahead of her. Yet she'd wed him only to keep the wolf at bay—one particularly vicious wolf. Tam was in fact naught but the lesser of two evils. Och, she might feel some affection toward him, having healed his hand, having taken him to her bed. Annie felt affection for most everyone in her world.

That was not love, the kind of love Tam now knew he felt for her—wide as a sea, strong as a storm wind, consuming as fire and unchanging as the rock beneath his feet.

Aye, he should have told her. Instead he stood here whinging while he might be finishing his chores.

Behind him, dutiful Sonsie did just that. She'd dragged out the wash kettle, and Tam had helped her haul water to fill it. Now she worked competently with the animals all around her and the house—far too silent—behind.

Tam should busy himself mucking out the byre and at least prove his worth as the worker Annie had hired.

Yet, just as he turned away from the gate, his eye caught a flash of movement down the lane. His heart leaped, only to fall once more an instant later. Not a cart, no, but a man on horseback, and a familiar figure at that.

As if Tam needed confirmation, Ruff rushed forward with a growl. "Randleigh," he muttered as if echoing the dog.

Sonsie looked up in dismay. "Och, nay!"

"Go inside," Tam told her. "Take the animals."

But there proved no time. Sonsie had not dried her hands before Randleigh reached the gate and hauled up his mount with cruel force.

He raked the farmyard with his gaze before asking Tam harshly, "Where is your wife? I need a word with her."

"Not here." Tam buried his fingers in the fur at Ruff's neck as the dog surged forward. Unfortunately, Ruff stood at his right side, and though those fingers now served far better than they had, he feared he might not be able to contain the animal. The hens had scattered at Randleigh's approach, the cat had slunk away, Fiona had run for the byre, and poor wee Ella shrank to Sonsie's side. But Ruff vibrated with defiance.

"Where is she? Off passing her remedies to the locals? Yes"—Randleigh glowered—"I know what she gets up to."

"'Tis naught to you where my wife may be."

That snared all Randleigh's attention and focused it on Tam. An ugly sneer distorted his features. "All high and mighty are you, thinking her standing will protect you? I tell you now, she can protect no one, including herself."

Tam stiffened. "How do you mean?"

"I have no call to explain myself to you. When your wife returns home, tell her I need a word with her about some rumors that have surfaced in the district. Tell her Laird Ardaugh has standards regarding those to whom he grants favors."

Tam narrowed his eyes, his mind racing.

Randleigh leaned over the gate into Tam's face. "Mind you deliver that message like a good hired man."

Taking exception to the factor's threatening movement, Ruff leaped, teeth snapping. Randleigh had his crop up at once—the same, no doubt, with which he'd thrashed Jockie.

"Curb that cur!" Randleigh snapped, and Ruff answered with a snarl, twisting from Tam's grip.

The crop came down. Sonsie screamed and Tam surged forward, putting himself between the dog and the blow. The crop took him across the face, leaving a blinding trail of pain.

"You'll not touch him," he growled. "Nor my wife."

"Then tell your wife to change her ways. I will not tolerate her defiance."

In a harsh movement Randleigh pulled his horse around and rode off the way he had come.

With a cry of dismay, Sonsie ran forward, Ella at her side.

"Master Tam! Och, sweet heaven, are you all right?"

Tam raised a hand to his face, far less than certain. Both dogs crowded close to him, Ruff gazing at him with almost human concern. "I do no' ken."

Sonsie gaped in horror. "Och, your face! He's near struck your eye. Here, come inside and let me clean it for you."

But Tam stood where he was, gazing down the path. "I wonder what he meant about Annie—what harm he means her."

"I do no' ken. He is gone for now, the boogle. Come along. I will use one of Miss Annie's remedies."

Remedies. The word echoed Randleigh's, and a dark chill of foreboding flooded Tam's heart.

****

Sonsie fretted the whole time she dressed Tam's injury, and both dogs remained close, Ella at his feet and the bigger dog with eyes fastened on the door.

"A hero you were, Master Tam," Sonsie declared as she pressed a cloth to his face. "Mistress Annie would ha' been that upset to find Ruff harmed—and I ha' no doubt that brute would have thrashed him even as he did our Jockie. Of course," the girl reflected, a thoughtful look in her hazel eyes, "she will no' be pleased to return and find you marked, either."

"How bad is it?" Tam asked. He had no looking glass but could feel the blow had taken him at an angle from his right temple to his left cheek, biting deep.

"Well," Sonsie scrutinized him again, "at least it caught but the corner o' your eye and so spared your sight. Does it hurt much?"

Tam grunted. He was used to pain. What worried

135

him far more was his fear on Annie's behalf. He had
failed once before to protect those he loved.

How did he suppose he might defend her now?

The sting of both that thought and his injury kept
him awake all night in Annie's big bed, aching for her.
He arose before the sun—before even Sonsie—and
went out into the yard. Both dogs accompanied him,
Ruff having apparently taken a place as his guardian
following yesterday's stance together. The yard still lay
dark, shrouded in mist and the fleeing night. But far to
the east—whence Annie had ridden—brightness bled
from the horizon. It seemed symbolic, as if all the light
in Tam's world lay with the Wee Crow, all strength
wrapped up in kindness and passion.

He needed to tell her how he felt for her, how he
loved her. He would, just as soon as she returned.

Yet what danger awaited her when she did? He
misliked the look in Randleigh's eye, and the
uneasiness that had accompanied him all night speared
him yet.

He went back inside to find Sonsie arisen.

"Keep the dogs here," he bade her. "I am going to
walk to Kirstie's and check on them."

"Why?" Sonsie's eyes went wide.

"Just a feeling I have."

"What if yon Randleigh comes back while you are
gone?"

"Stay inside and do no' answer the door to him. I
will return as soon as I can."

"What of your breakfast?"

"Never mind that. Just keep the door barred."

"Take Ruff with you," Sonsie urged, but Tam
shook his head.

He would not risk the dog; Annie loved him far too well.

Chapter Twenty

Dawn spread across the sky and the light strengthened as Tam went over the brae at a jog, all his senses on alert. Curious how alive he felt, as if something inside him—banked like a fire since the deaths of his parents—had awakened, returned to life. Had Annie begun to heal more than his hand?

Longing for her filled him, pushing aside the helpless anger that had accompanied him all winter. Aye, the anger lingered, but it now had to contest for space with the love in his heart.

Over the brae and through the dawn mist he ran, and heard the furor even before he reached Kirstie's croft—raised voices, one of them that of a woman protesting something. He breasted the hill and beheld the scene.

Men and horses crowded the lane outside Kirstie's gate—Tam hastily counted four horses and as many men. Randleigh stood with his hand on the latch and the other three, all dismounted, at his back.

Inside the yard, Jockie—looking a fright made of welts and fair hair—faced off against them all, with Kirstie doing her best to intervene. Tam saw why; Randleigh once more had his crop in hand. Like the lass, Tam doubted Jockie could endure another thrashing.

"Randleigh!" Tam bellowed in an effort to distract

the factor, even as the man raised the crop high.

The factor and his men all spun. Who were Randleigh's companions? Hired henchmen? Workers from the laird's estate? And why did Randleigh suppose he needed them at his back? Surely he did not fear one lone, injured lad?

Not lone now. Tam leaped the wall and went to stand at Jockie's side.

"Keep away, Sutherland. This has nothing to do with you."

Even as he spoke, Randleigh pushed through the gate. Jockie, who held a pitchfork before him like a staff, edged Kirstie aside, his message clear; Randleigh would have to go through him to reach the lass.

Kirstie protested again and threw her arms around Jockie. Tam moved to put himself between the two of them and Randleigh.

"Move aside," the factor ordered. "Did you not have enough yesterday?"

Consumed with rage, Tam embraced the strength of the emotion. "What goes on here?"

"We have come to take Jock MacCallum into custody." Randleigh nodded at his men.

"For what?"

"Attacking me."

"What? 'Twas you attacked him. Only look at the lad."

"I merely acted in self-defense when he went off his head and tried to throttle me. Everyone in the district knows he is mad."

"Would you go so far," Tam challenged, "to get what you want? Do these men know why they are here?" Tam shot a look at the men who stood behind the factor. "He wants the lass, and Jock MacCallum is in his way."

"Move aside, I say, Sutherland, unless you wish to appear before the magistrate also."

Tam did not. In his experience, magistrates, appointed from the local gentry, tended to be in the landowners' pockets. Yet he said, "You will no' take him."

Several things happened in swift succession. Randleigh, already halfway through the gate, raised his crop. Tam snatched the pitchfork from Jockie and leaped forward. The men at Randleigh's back surged in.

The ensuing fray, intense and furious and punctuated by Kirstie's cries and the sound of blows, lasted until she managed to pull Jockie away and Randleigh's three henchmen wrestled Tam to the ground. He did not go easily and still had Randleigh's sneering face in his sights when his back hit the dirt.

Two of the factor's henchmen pinned Tam's arms, while the third knelt on his chest, all breathless.

Randleigh, with fire in his eyes, declared, "You all witnessed this man attack me with intent to do grievous harm. He shall be taken into custody and held until the magistrate can deal with him."

"Nay!" Kirstie cried, but only because Jockie started forward to Tam's aid. The girl wrapped her arms more closely about the lad and hauled him back with all her might.

Randleigh fixed Jockie with a cold eye. "Do you want to share his prison? Then count your blessings I do not arrest you also."

"This is an injustice!" Tam hollered from his place on the ground. "You canno' use the law to your own ends—"

"No?" Randleigh leaned over him. "We shall see."

Tam spat curses, hurling his hate with the words, and Randleigh's face twisted with ugly emotion.

"You, Sutherland, are far too full of yourself for a landless, crippled peasant. What happened to that hand of yours, by the way? Fingers twisted—appears as if they were all broken."

Deliberately, Randleigh stepped across to where his man held Tam's wrist to the ground. Tam saw his black-booted foot move and realized what he intended a moment before it descended on his hand. The factor's weight followed, crushing Tam's splayed fingers. Randleigh pressed deliberately and ground the hand into the hard soil.

Tam did not want to holler—would not give the bastard the satisfaction—yet pain surged up his arm and burned a path to his brain and tore a strangled cry from his throat.

Kirstie cried out also, her voice a sharper echo of Tam's, and began to weep, still holding Jockie as for her life.

Red and black dots danced before Tam's eyes before Randleigh removed his weight.

"Bring him," he snapped. "The man is clearly dangerous."

****

"Thank you, Rory, for your company and all your efforts. I am sorry it did no' give us a better result."

"Aye." Rory MacBain's craggy face looked as woeful as Annie felt. "Well, mistress, you did give it a good try. No one can say differently. Good night."

"The same to you."

Annie turned from the gate, her heart every bit as heavy as the horses' weary feet. All day long they had traveled. Now night drew down, and with what she could only consider abject failure behind her, she had one intense longing: to see her husband and take refuge in his arms.

She started up the walk, and a shadow emerged from the side window—Sol coming to greet her. The door flew open an instant later, and those she loved emerged in a group—Sonsie and the animals, with Ruff at the fore. Jockie, of course, would still be at Kirstie's. But where was Tam?

"Miss!" Sonsie cried with a strange note in her voice. "Och, I am so glad you are home."

"What is amiss?"

Annie stopped where she stood, and Sonsie met her halfway. Ella, a mere ball of white in the near-dark, hurled herself at Annie's ankles, and Ruff pressed close, trembling.

Ruff, trembling? Annie sought Sonsie's eyes. "Sonsie, what—? Where is my husband?"

"Taken." Tears accompanied the bleak word and emotion twisted Sonsie's features.

"What?"

"Randleigh." Sonsie spat the word like an epithet. "He and his men went to Kirstie's today. Master Tam tried to help her and Jockie, but they took him into custody. Och, and hurt him so terribly—"

Annie felt the blood drain from her face, and her stomach twisted violently. "Hurt him? How?"

"Kirstie says they wrestled him down, pinned his hand and— Och, his poor hand…"

"Nay!" Annie swayed where she stood, as if she

felt Tam's pain. Sonsie reached for her arm. "Where? Where have they taken him?"

"I do no' ken. The laird's house? Kirstie did not know. She came running to tell me after it happened, she near drowning in tears."

Annie gathered up her bag and headed for the house. "Was anyone else hurt?"

"Nay, just affrighted. Master Tam—he defended them."

Aye, so, and the one-handed leftover hireling had proved a lion in his defense of what Annie loved. She swayed again, her hand on the house door, facing a terrible reality. She could not—simply could not!—bear to lose him.

"Miss?" Sonsie paused beside her. "What will you do?"

Annie gazed into the girl's eyes. "I will go there and speak for him, see can I win him free."

"But, miss, do you no' see that is likely what Randleigh wants? He maun see this as his opportunity to…to force you."

"I canno' help that." Randleigh had taken her heart; what could she do but follow?

Chapter Twenty-One

Sonsie did not want to let Annie go to the laird's house alone.

"Let me come wi' you," she begged as Annie hurriedly changed into clean clothing and gulped down a cup of hot broth.

Annie shook her head. The way she saw it, she'd already put Tam at risk with terrible consequences. "Stay you here, love, and keep the animals safe."

Working together, the girl and the woman led Old Rake from his stall and harnessed him to the cart, usually one of Jockie's duties. The laird's property lay a fair distance south and east, too far for Annie to walk quickly.

"What will you do when you get there?" Sonsie asked.

"Try and talk him free."

Sonsie grimaced, revealing her doubt—a full measure of which emotion already occupied Annie's heart alongside the desperate fear. Returning and finding Tam gone had brought a few things home to her, made it impossible to deny her feelings for him. What a strange twist of fate that she should have gone to the hiring fair for the sake of those who relied on her, only to find the other half of her own heart.

Yet as her mother always said, there were no coincidences in this life.

"Miss?" Sonsie touched her hand. "You will be careful?"

"I will."

"And—I canno' believe I forgot to ask—were you successful wi' the laird?"

Annie shook her head somberly. "Nay, Sonsie."

"Ah, well—better luck now."

It could scarcely be worse.

****

"Where is my husband?"

Annie stood at the door of the parlor and delivered the query with all the force she could muster. It had been a long while since she'd visited Laird Ardaugh's home, and she could not but think how things here had changed. The place felt bleak and cold; outside, Randleigh's henchmen seemed very much in evidence. To her dismay, she'd been forced to leave Old Rake with one of them.

And now she found Ned Randleigh sprawled in the laird's armchair as if he owned the place, sitting in his shirtsleeves with the firelight leaping across his features, making him look very like Annie's idea of a demon. Who did the man think he was?

He did not bother to rise when Annie came in but looked up at her and smiled the kind of smile a corpse might grin after six months in the ground.

A slow chill traced its way up Annie's spine, and all at once she knew Sonsie was right—she'd been a fool to come here alone. Her presence had been Randleigh's true objective.

"Ah, Mistress MacCallum. But I err—it is Mistress Sutherland now."

"It is. Tell me, do you hold Tam Sutherland here?

And for what reason?"

"I do. The man attacked me, proving himself dangerous and aggressive."

"I do no' believe it."

"Oh, you may believe it, Mistress Sutherland. Such defiance cannot be tolerated and, I assure you, will not go unpunished."

Annie trembled both within and without. "What have you done to him?"

"Nothing beyond my rights—surely even you must admit I have just cause to defend myself against an unruly tenant." Randleigh got to his feet slowly. "But he is not my tenant, is he? You are."

"I am Laird Ardaugh's tenant," Annie spat, "not yours." All her instincts flared to life as Randleigh moved toward her. "You are but his hired agent."

"And as such I hold authority to act in his stead—just as if I were him. Do you ken, mistress, that in days gone by, Highland chiefs sometimes took liberties with their female tenants? I have studied on it. And you, being an educated woman, must be aware of your history."

"Not all lairds, certainly no' Laird Ardaugh. Anyway, all that was a long time ago."

"Was it? I would not be so quick to dismiss the practice, if I were you. You have so little with which to bargain."

Annie met his gaze and took a decided step backward. "You are a vile and disgraceful excuse for a man, Ned Randleigh."

"But far better, I think, than you've already had—if you let that broken-down croft worker into your bed. Why, he can't even read and write. And that hand of his—hopelessly crippled."

Annie's stomach clenched violently. "I ask again, what ha' you done to him?"

Still ignoring the question, Randleigh took another step closer. Annie realized he had been drinking. The laird's good Scotch, no doubt.

"He is being held here in a strong room until the magistrate can deal with him."

"I mean his hand—" Annie's throat closed.

"He fought with me and my men and had to be subdued. It is not my fault if he was injured during that struggle."

"Has he been tended by a physician? Let me see him."

"You, Mistress Sutherland, are not a physician, though you do dabble in cures and potions, don't you? A right risky undertaking, some might say."

"Potions? What are you talking about?"

"I am aware of what you get up to in the district. You are the local wise woman—a witch."

Annie shied from the word, one her mother had always avoided for fear of its negative connotations.

"Nay," she denied.

Randleigh feigned a thoughtful frown. "I have heard the rumors. Do the women hereabouts not flock to you for charms, predictions of the future…spells?"

"Spells?" Annie faltered. "Nay."

Randleigh's narrow lips twisted in distaste. "Tea leaf reading, I believe…" He paused. "And other magic."

"It is no' magic," Annie denied. More like faith, but she could not hope to make such a man as this understand.

"Still"—he tipped his head in a terrible parody of consideration—"a dangerous charge, I am thinking. I quite grasp that the role of a seer is well-accepted here in the Highlands. Yet in days gone by, witches were burned at the stake."

Another step took him still closer; he now stood far too near for Annie's comfort. "What you need, Mistress Sutherland, is not a half-crippled farmhand but a protector, a man who can see that all such charges fall away from you."

Annie sucked in a breath that scorched her throat, and her thoughts raced wildly. She stood on a quaking bog and needed to choose most carefully just where to step.

"I am a married woman."

"Are you? True, the priest performed the rite, but you and I both know it for a mere ruse on your part. This 'husband' of yours can be dealt with, eliminated."

"How?"

Again Randleigh smiled. "There are ways. If it can be proven he threatened my life more than once, he could hang. Or there is transportation to Australia. He would be as good as dead to you then."

Annie's dismay must have shown on her face, for Randleigh continued, "Do not look so uncertain. He is unworthy of you—an ignorant peasant. You wish to protect the people of this district, do you not? To suspend the clearings and keep them in their homes? You and I might strike a bargain to benefit all."

Annie's stomach turned. "A bargain," she repeated warily.

"Allow me to dispense with the unfortunate complication of your husband. Then you can come here to me even as I once asked and you refused. I will show mercy to the folks under Laird Ardaugh's care."

And what about her, Annie? Would he show her mercy also, in his bed? She had seen how he used Kirstie, and it was the Devil's bargain.

"Let me think on it," she breathed. "Meanwhile, I wish to see my husband."

"That is not possible."

She glared into his eyes. "Either I see him here and now or there will be no consideration for your offer."

"My generous offer."

Annie said nothing but somehow managed to hold his gaze.

"Very well, I will allow you a few minutes with him, no more. But I will have your answer in three days—by the time the magistrate comes. Understand?"

Annie nodded stiffly.

Randleigh leaned toward her, and the smell of whisky assaulted her nostrils. "You know you could have given me your assent in the first place and saved everyone this trouble. Stupid woman."

****

Night had come again, the darkness settling down like a blanket, and Tam once more struggled to control his anger and frustration. He could see very little beyond the walls of the small room where Randleigh had confined him. He had very nearly lost track of the time, as well; he knew only that it had been far too long.

But every so often the door opened to reveal an armed man who pushed in a small measure of food and water, not enough to keep him satisfied. He knew he must eat, though the poor fare nearly choked him.

Instinct alone bade him stay alive.

He suspected death would be easier.

Yet he needed to stay alive, if only in hopes of seeing Annie again.

Her essence kept him company just like the pain in his hand. His hand—much of his rage stemmed from what Randleigh had done to him, even though he knew very well the rage could not serve him now.

He believed more than one of his fingers had broken beneath Randleigh's heel, all the magical healing Annie had achieved undone. Hatred, hot and bright, flared in his heart. He'd once believed the factor who had caused the death of his parents the cruelest and most abhorrent man walking the earth; Ned Randleigh now supplanted him. If Tam had but a few moments with the bastard at his mercy, even his ruined hand would not keep him from meting out fit justice.

Upon that thought he heard a sound at the door and stiffened in every limb. He'd already had his supper, such as it was. Who would be coming now? It could not be good news for him.

Yet the door swung open to reveal a miracle.

Chapter Twenty-Two

"Tam…" Annie spoke his name and distinctly felt her heart break into a hundred separate pieces. Tears flooded her eyes, and she choked them back desperately. She refused to let Ned Randleigh see her weep.

But this man she loved—and she could no longer deny how completely she did love him—looked like a caged beast, harshly confined. Always there had been a certain hard-held, native dignity about Tam Sutherland despite his reduced circumstances and ruined hand. It had been one of the things she first noticed about him at the hiring fair.

That dignity endured yet, aye, visible in his eyes and the set of his shoulders, but wildly eroded by desperation and pain.

Annie tore her gaze from him and turned to the man who loomed behind her, a dark presence. "I wish to speak with him alone."

"That was not part of our bargain. You asked only to see him."

"It has now become part of our bargain, unless you wish me to dismiss the rest of your offer from my consideration."

Randleigh grunted but stepped back and shut the door of the prison, locking Annie inside. She clearly heard the rattle of the lock.

The strong room, as he'd called it, must have been used as a prison before; no more than eight paces by eight, it afforded no comforts save one thin blanket and a chamber pot. A narrow window high up on the wall admitted but a breath of air and a scrap of night sky.

She raised her eyes to Tam's and reached for him with her hands. "Och, your face—what has he done to you?"

"That is naught." Tam had sprung up from the floor and now stood as if rooted, with that terrible anguish filling his eyes. He visibly fought his emotions before he said, "Annie, by God, what are you doing here? You should never ha' come."

"I had to. As soon as I heard—"

"He has no' harmed you?"

"Nay." She shook her head. *Not yet.*

"What did he mean about you making a bargain wi' him? Tell me you ha' not given that beast a hold over you."

Annie shook her head.

"Promise you will not. For I ken fine what he wants from you—"

"Hush." Annie stepped forward into his arms, lifted her face, and kissed him, driven by the wild, tangled emotions in her heart. Each moment away from him she'd longed for this. Now, together again, she could do nothing other than follow the irresistible impulse.

His lips responded to hers avidly, claiming and consuming. For the space of a hundred heartbeats, time suspended and all fears flew away. No need for words, no room for doubt. Then Annie drew away from him— not far—and caught his face between her hands.

"Och, Tam, Tam—what happened?"

"Never mind me. Did you succeed in persuading the laird? Will he set the bastard aside?"

The tears in Annie's eyes spilled over. "I did no' see the laird." All those long, difficult miles, all the things she'd planned to say, for naught.

"He was no' there?"

"He was, but too ill to see me, so they said. I saw his clerk, a man named Barnes, who seems to be in charge of the household there. But no matter how I argued and persuaded, he would no' let me see Laird Ardaugh." Aye, she had argued—and begged. "In the end I had to satisfy myself wi' writing another letter, which Master Barnes promised to give to him." But she had not been satisfied—not a bit. "Tam, what happened to make Randleigh imprison you?"

Tam took a half step back, though he kept her within the circle of his arms. "He was at Kirstie's, hell bent on flogging Jock again—and worse. I tried to intervene. But he had men wi' him. They pinned me down and—"

"And, what?"

Pain flickered in Tam's eyes. "My hand."

"Your hand." Gently and determinedly, she caught it up in both hers. Tears flooded her vision once more when she saw his fingers, crushed and swollen, surely denoting broken bones.

"Och!" For an instant rage stole her ability to say more. She choked it back somehow. "The monster! And he's left you like this? No care, no physician?"

Tam set his jaw. "Nay."

"I need to get you awa' out of here, clean those abrasions, set the bones if I can…" Aye, and what if the only way she could accomplish that meant agreeing to

Randleigh's demands? Was there no other hope of getting Tam free?

His good hand tightened on her shoulder. "You ha' no' told me of this bargain he wants."

Annie dared not share that with him, not given the frustration she could see in his eyes. He just might go wild and do himself further injury.

"Never mind that now. List to me, Tam—you maun stay calm as you can, marshal your strength until I can win you free."

"Win me free? How? He means to stand me before the magistrate, who will surely take his part. You know how it is for the likes o' me."

"You need to claim self-defense."

"'Twill no' matter what I claim. The magistrate will be in Laird Ardaugh's pocket, and thus Randleigh's."

"I am no' so sure the laird knows what Randleigh has been getting up to."

"But you wrote to him—"

"Aye, but I do not know that he read my first letter or will read this one I just wrote. Randleigh says the magistrate will no' be available to hear your case for three days. I will make sure and be there when Randleigh stands you before him. Meanwhile I will do all I can to get a physician sent in—or persuade him to let me back in to tend you."

"How do you mean to persuade him?" Even in the poor light Annie could see the bleak devastation in Tam's gray eyes. "I ken fine what he wants from you. Annie, you are not to agree, not for any cause."

"Let me worry about that."

"Nay—you listen to me, now. I will no' have you

even consider it! Bad enough what he has already done to me. But for me to be unable to protect you—" His throat worked violently. "I was unable to protect those dear to me once before. I will no' let it happen again."

Those dear to him? Did he include her, Annie, in that number? Yet he'd never told her he loved her, even though, aye, she fancied she'd felt it in the tenderness of his touch, the warmth of his kiss.

All her words stolen, she said nothing, and he hurried on. "Annie lass, I ken fine how you are—far too apt to sacrifice yourself for others. I will no' have you endanger yoursel' for me. I am no' worth it."

Her lips trembled. "You are."

"Nay." He shook his head violently. "I am no one of consequence. You, though, have a full life and many people depending on you."

"But," Annie said helplessly, "I depend on *you*." Until she spoke the words she did not realize just how true they were. More softly she added, "So I have come to do, ever since that first day I laid eyes on you."

She raised his injured hand very gently and placed a tender kiss on the palm. "Stay strong for me, Tam, and we will come through this together—so I do promise."

"Not at the price of your—"

The door behind Annie opened abruptly, and the two of them started. Randleigh stood there, a hard look on his face.

"Enough. My indulgence is at an end."

"My husband needs a physician. I demand—"

"You demand?" Randleigh raked Annie with a scornful look. "Who are you to demand anything? You are a tenant, like the rest of those who infest Laird

Ardaugh's holdings…just better educated—and better looking—than most."

Tam bristled, and Annie stayed him with a hand on his arm. He had already suffered enough on her account.

She lifted her chin. "If I send a physician, do you agree to admit him? If not, I will no' consider your other request."

"What—" Tam began again.

Randleigh interrupted him. "Aye, but it must be a genuine physician, mind—none of your old women's spells and potions."

"Agreed. And you will let me send in food."

"I will not. I have said it is enough. Step away from the prisoner."

Annie attempted yet again, "But I think that—"

"Mistress Sutherland, you have already had far more leeway from me than you deserve. Would you prefer me to change my mind about the physician?"

Annie withdrew her hand from Tam's arm and stepped to the door. She longed to look back at him but hated to give Randleigh the satisfaction.

They went out, and she watched Randleigh lock the door.

If only she might overpower him here and now. If she did in truth possess some dark spell she might employ against him—but her mother had taught her none. Would she use such power if she could? Just like Randleigh's poor excuse for mercy, it carried a price she did not want to pay.

Yet leaving Tam Sutherland alone and in pain fair killed her.

Randleigh smiled at her in the dim corridor. "Make

up your mind swiftly, Mistress Sutherland, whether you will save him or no. You will not wish to leave him languishing long."

Somehow Annie found the courage to glare into his eyes. "Have a care, Ned Randleigh: the harm you do will come back on you threefold. Remember that, even as you unleash your cruelty."

Chapter Twenty-Three

"Och, miss, what will you do?" The corners of Sonsie's misshapen mouth turned down and her hands fluttered in distress. "You simply canno' give in to that beast's demands."

"Nay," Kirstie agreed firmly.

"Nay," Jockie grunted, his pale blue eyes blazing.

The four of them, including Kirstie, huddled together over the table in Annie's kitchen, meeting for what felt very much like a council of war. Morning had come, drear and wet to match Annie's mood. And she had told these three the truth about Randleigh's demands. Why hide it from them? Kirstie, of all people, knew the depth of the man's cruelty.

She tangled her fingers together and said slowly, "I canno' just let Tam languish there, can I? His hand…" Her throat closed abruptly when she thought of him suffering alone, and because of her. She had dragged him into this situation; she'd endangered him.

"Aye, but," Sonsie said quickly, "you canno' pay such a price."

Annie raised eyes awash with tears to each of them in turn. "I love Tam Sutherland," she declared simply. "I never meant for it to happen. When all this began, I could no' have dreamed it. But he is inside me now, and I can no sooner abandon him than my breath."

Sonsie looked down at her hands. Kirstie and

Jockie exchanged swift glances.

"Ah, now," Kirstie said. "Such feelings can well develop when a woman welcomes a man to her bed."

All Annie's instincts went on alert. She studied Kirstie's face and then Jock's. Kirstie and Jockie? Surely not. But aye, she had seen Kirstie's tender way with him after Randleigh's attack. And even now a flush warmed the lass's face, while Jockie looked steadier and more certain than she'd ever seen him, a man rather than a boy.

Well, well… Annie's heart lifted in joy for them despite her own misery. No wonder Jock had refused to come home.

He leaned across the table and covered Annie's hand with his fingers. His face, only partially healed, still bore livid welts, but his eyes burned.

He fought to marshal his words. "You ha' been good to me, miss, when no one else was. Your uncle and your ma and you took me in and treated me well."

Annie answered truthfully, "You are like a brother to me, Jockie."

"Aye. That is why you maun let me help you now, you and your love."

The simple sincerity of the words touched Annie deeply, but she said, "I do no' want you involved in this. Randleigh already has his eye on you. He will take any excuse to hurt you again."

"Randleigh." Jockie spat the word.

"Stay out of it," Annie advised.

"But," Sonsie argued, "you canno' fight this battle alone. Folks throughout the district will surely aid you, after all you ha' done for them."

"And give Randleigh an excuse to move on with

the clearances? He has only held his hand this long for the power it gives him." Annie thought about the expression on Randleigh's face at the laird's house and his sly smile. "He enjoys holding such power over others and bending them to his will." Indeed, perhaps that even more than the act itself led him to force the women at his mercy. "If folks hereabouts defy him and come to my aid, he will carry out the threat he has held over us for so long."

"You could speak to the magistrate," Sonsie suggested. "Make your plea to him ahead of Randleigh."

"I can try. Laird Donaldson over at Strathmore was appointed magistrate last year. He never knew my uncle or my mother. But Randleigh spoke as if he were unavailable—'tis part of the reason he gave me time."

Kirstie returned, "He gave you time in order to watch you squirm." She glanced at Jockie again. "Sometimes I think 'twould be better to just up and leave, go to Canada as so many others have. If my grandmother would agree to stir, I just might."

Leave here—not for a day or a fortnight but forever? Annie didn't know if she could. Like those of Kirstie's old grandmother, her roots ran deep in this soil, her wellbeing flowing with the seasons, her spirit tethered to the hills. Leaving would be like cutting out her heart.

Yet Kirstie spoke true: so many had already gone, and if the clearances continued, many more would follow. Sheep would take their places, their lonely cries echoing where once there was laughter and song.

"Opportunity waits in Canada," Kirstie maintained, "and no cruel factor coming to the door."

Jockie looked at her thoughtfully, and Annie's heart trembled still more violently. Might she lose him? Yet he, grown now, in truth, had a right to his own choices and a chance at a future.

But Jockie shook his ragged towhead and fought to speak again. "Kill him," he forced out. "Break into laird's house. Kill Randleigh—break Tam free."

Kirstie exclaimed in dismay, and Annie shook her head.

"Nay, Jock—I canno' let you attempt such a thing. 'Tis never right to choose violence."

"Nay?" he returned surprisingly. "Yet you canno' stay me."

Desperately Annie said, "Tell him, Kirstie—'twill be a course to ruin. He would face the noose or deportation." The very same fate that awaited Tam.

Kirstie bit her lip. "Your kindness does you credit, miss, but a man as evil as Randleigh deserves to die."

"'Tis no' up to us to decide what he deserves. And to be sure, Jockie does no' deserve a life spent in a penal colony." Deported—from all she'd heard, it truly was a fate more terrible than death.

Her thoughts flew to Tam, shut into the tiny room where she'd last seen him, trapped with his anger and pain.

"For now, I need to locate a physician. Jock, if I write a letter, will you take it to Strathmore for me? I believe there is a physician in residence there."

"How will you pay?" asked Sonsie, ever practical.

"I have a few coins." Very few. "Pray it will be enough."

****

"Miss, a word?"

Afternoon had come, struggling through rain and mist, gloomy as the morning. Jockie and Old Rake had gone off westward, bearing Annie's letter of plea to the physician. But Kirstie had lingered, waiting, Annie thought, for Jock's return. Yet as soon as Sonsie busied herself in the yard, Kirstie approached Annie.

"What is it?" Annie, deep in worrisome thoughts, struggled to put her own concerns aside and listen.

Kirstie sat down at the table. "You know so much about things, miss—some I will never understand. Do you ken the nature o' Jockie's affliction?"

That snagged all Annie's attention. "Not much," she said frankly. "He came to us as a young lad, you ken. You must ha' heard the story." Though Kirstie would have been very young also when Uncle Dennis rescued Jockie from life in that cage.

Kirstie nodded gravely. "So 'tis true, then? His own people used him that way?"

"I do not know they were his people. Tinkers and other travelers often snatch children for their own purposes."

"Poor lad. But what made him the way he is? Folks 'round here whisper 'twas dark magic, but I am fair certain whatever afflicts him, 'tis no' the Devil, for his heart is too good."

Annie shrugged helplessly. To be sure, Annie's mother and uncle had sometimes pondered the matter in hushed voices. She did not know if her mother, for all her wisdom, had reached a conclusion. Jockie's problems were manifold and affected his body rather than his mind. His right side, though slightly stunted, appeared normal—the left, twisted, had never grown aright. And though his thoughts moved swiftly, he could not easily express them.

Kirstie, a slight flush on her cheek, went on, "I ha' found he can speak more readily when he is at ease. 'Tis as if when he stops trying to force the words, they can come from him." The girl met Annie's wondering gaze a bit defiantly. "Such times as when we are abed together after…after…"

"I see."

In a rush, Kirstie said, "I never expected for it to happen. But he was so good to me, so brave. So sweet. And 'tis not all about how a man looks, is it? 'Tis about what lies in his heart."

Aye, and if only Annie could be sure Tam Sutherland believed that.

"Only"—Kirstie leaned closer—"what concerns me now is, this trouble that afflicts Jockie, could it be passed to a bairn?"

"Kirstie, lass, are you telling me you are—"

"Nay. At least, not yet. I am thankful to say I ha' not got that monster Randleigh's bairn, at least. But if we keep on—well, Jockie is healthy enough that way, if you ken what I mean."

"Och, well…" Life never stopped delivering surprises. "Kirstie, I canno' answer your question. I tend to think, as my mother did, that somewhat went wrong when Jockie was born. My mother said that happens sometimes when a woman's labor is overlong and difficult. But I ha' no certain answers for you—I simply do no' ken."

Kirstie's face lit. "Yet Jockie's bairn might be right and healthy."

"Aye, Kirstie, but have a care." Annie laid her hand on the girl's arm. "'Twould be ill indeed to let

Randleigh get wind of you bedding Jock. I do no' suppose that man would take well to Jockie having what is now denied to him."

Chapter Twenty-Four

Two days later, Annie traveled to the laird's house once again, this time in the company of a physician. Master Camden, a sour-faced man in a rusty black frock coat, had demanded his payment up front and made no secret of the fact that he disliked the idea of treating a prisoner. But at least, in answer to Annie's letter, pleading and persuading, he had come.

Now he stared down his long nose at her and said, "Your letter did not advise me we would have a further journey. Nor did your servant."

"Does it matter?" Annie challenged. "Are you no' sworn to alleviate suffering wherever you find it? Besides, my husband is falsely accused and being held unjustly. He has no' seen the magistrate, nor has he been convicted."

Camden snorted. But he stopped his complaining once they arrived and Annie faced off with Ned Randleigh again, at last gaining admittance to the strong room. As soon as the physician saw Tam's hand and his general condition, which had worsened mightily since Annie had been with him, he went silent, a new gravity in his eyes.

With Randleigh standing by, he performed a thorough examination, questioned Tam about the origin of his injuries, and inquired as to how he had been treated since being taken into custody.

Tam, pulling no punches, told it plainly, a sheen of perspiration caused by pain on his skin.

"I would I had seen this injury sooner," Camden said then, after taking a long look at Ned Randleigh. "You have at least three broken bones in that hand, and they have all begun to set—badly, I am afraid."

"What can you do for him?" Annie asked.

"The best course now is to rebreak the fingers and then attempt to set them properly. It will be very painful, and I cannot do it here. I will need more room—air and light."

Faced down by the physician, Randleigh allowed them to repair to the dining room under guard, where Annie witnessed one of the most horrific procedures she had ever seen. Tam kept from hollering, no doubt refusing to give Randleigh—in the next room—the satisfaction. But Annie did not know how.

Afterwards, with a hard look at Tam and another at the guards, Camden said, "I advise this patient be given a strong tot of whisky. Where is his jailer?"

As Annie suspected, Randleigh had been listening and came in with the familiar sneer on his face.

The physician gave him a scathing glare. "Is it true, sir, that you caused this man's injuries and then left them untreated?"

"Not quite; the prisoner exaggerates."

"No exaggeration that those broken fingers should have been set properly days ago. Why is this man being held in these conditions?"

"He attacked me and now awaits justice."

"I shall return in two days to reexamine him, and he'd better be in good condition then—bandaging clean and no signs of further ill use. Do you understand, sir?"

Randleigh blanched. "I do."

"Good. It is unconscionable to leave even an animal in such pain."

Randleigh said nothing, but he shot a look at Annie that told her, *You will pay for this.*

The physician continued, "Why has he been held so long without facing a magistrate?"

"The magistrate is away," Randleigh replied shortly, and added to his men, "Put the prisoner back in the strong room."

"Please," Annie spoke swiftly, "if I might have another moment with him—"

"You have had enough favors from me," Randleigh growled. "Put him back, I say."

Annie, tears in her eyes, had to satisfy herself with exchanging a long look with Tam as he was hauled away.

As she turned back to Randleigh, the physician asked, "Who is laird here?"

Sourly, Randleigh replied, "Laird Ardaugh MacCallum."

"And you are his hired agent?"

"I am—and with full authority."

"Where is the laird now?"

"In Edinburgh," Annie replied. "I ha' been to see him just recently."

That earned her another dangerous glare from Randleigh, and she wondered if Tam would suffer for it once she and the physician had gone.

"I shall return," Camden reminded the factor. "Fair treatment, mind."

When they went outside, the physician paused and eyed Annie. "A most unpleasant man, the factor."

"Aye, sir." He had no idea.

"Give me your laird's direction—I will write and inform him of what I have observed here."

"Och, would you?" Annie's heart struggled to rise. "I would appreciate it ever so much."

"As you so aptly pointed out, mistress, I am sworn to alleviate suffering in whatever way I can. Did your husband attack that man?"

"Nay, sir—he but got in the way when Master Randleigh sought to harm another."

The physician grunted. "I will meet you here in two days, at ten of the clock."

For the first time in days, a ray of hope pierced the darkness in Annie's heart. "Thank you, Master Camden."

****

Tam lay flat upon the floor of his prison, watching the sliver of light that was all he could see through his window. Since the physician's visit, the pain in his hand had slowly abated from a raging storm to a steady throb, yet the storm in his heart refused to quiet. He wanted to throw himself at the door and walls of his prison, shout out his anger. Remaining quiet required self-discipline he'd never suspected he possessed.

He hated this helplessness, had believed he'd reached the height of that emotion the night he watched his mother die. But seeing Annie and beholding the agony in her dark eyes, knowing he could do nothing to ease it, felt almost worse.

He could scarcely bear to think what Randleigh might ask of her for his, Tam's, sake. As he'd told her, he now understood her capacity for self-sacrifice.

He'd wanted to shout at her when the physician

came, forbid her to pay Randleigh's price—to let him rot here in this room if he must. He was not worth her spending all her warmth, her caring, her dignity.

He could say none of those things now, so he thought of her instead—lay with his eyes on the light and remembered each individual moment they had shared.

The first time he saw her moving about the fair clad in her green cloak and gown, the broad-brimmed hat with Sol's feather sweeping down to her cheek…the first time their eyes met and the sheer life he'd encountered, dark and curious as the gaze of a crow. Wee Crow—the name suited her, for she possessed vast and fundamental wisdom.

With all the things she knew, did she know she owned his heart? Nay, for fool that he was he had failed to tell her, not even when he held her in his arms.

Fresh memories found him then: the first time they had kissed, the warmth of it like homecoming, the power of it like flame. The first time she'd welcomed him to her bed, taking his ruined hand into her hands, taking his ruined life, as well…and every smile, every word, each exchanged glance since then…

He lay sore and hurting and relived it all, exquisite torture and comfort combined.

The woman possessed magic, far more than she knew. Enough to reunite them?

His heart said aye, his reason argued nay. Then, outside his narrow window, he heard the call of a crow, sharp and persistent, speaking to him—calling up his courage and his faith.

There alone, wrapped in despair, he smiled.

Chapter Twenty-Five

Annie lit the candles one by one, each at a cardinal point in the circle: east, south, west, and north. She closed her eyes and breathed deeply, envisioning the circle of protection that linked the flames and surrounded her.

White magic. She'd been raised on it and believed in it to the very root of her soul. Her connection to this power that flowed from the earth and through every element in her world was fundamental to her existence, and she invoked those powers every time she whispered a prayer or prepared a charm on someone's behalf.

Yet never before had she asked anything for herself. Oh, aye, she had sued for strength when she needed it, especially after the losses of her mother and uncle. She'd asked for wisdom, the ability to alleviate pain, for endurance, and a solution to the problem Ned Randleigh represented. She'd begged for courage when she climbed onto the platform at the hiring fair.

Now, though, she came asking for Tam Sutherland, whom she needed desperately.

How had the man got so deep inside of her? She who had never expected to give her heart, having seen all the inherent perils too clearly, had lost that to him even before her maidenhead.

Now, part of her remained with him, languished in his prison even as the rest of her reached wildly for any available means to help him—including magic.

Aye, but she needed to keep her motives pure. Such powers demanded the strictest ethics, so her mother had taught. Any ill will led one down a perilous path into darkness.

But sitting here within the circle of light she found it harder than ever before to separate her intentions and her desires.

Outside, the evening drew down swiftly, dusk falling like a black cloak. On the morrow, the physician would return; on the morrow, if she meant to bargain for Tam's freedom, she would have to deliver her answer to Ned Randleigh.

Her whole being ached for Tam, for the sight of his smile, the sound of his voice at her ear in the dark. She craved his kiss and the way they'd laughed together. The sensation of his skin beneath her lips, the surging strength of him when he entered her.

Man and woman, a complete circle just like this circle in which she sat. And when love was involved, every bit as sacred.

How dared Randleigh suppose he could sully that, demand her body as the price of her love? Anger flared again and chased the clear serenity she needed to accomplish her goal. For she must have help; she simply could not do this alone.

Again she fought down her emotions and reached out with her mind. Sol, sensing her turmoil, fluttered his wings as if he would fly off out the window. Yet, very like a guardian, he remained.

I call upon the powers of the air, the fire, the water, and the earth to aid me this night. I need to win my Tam free and defeat Ned Randleigh.

Just reciting Randleigh's name threatened to destroy her concentration. Very rarely did she allow herself to taste the power of hatred; its intensity shocked her now. Yet when she thought on the things Randleigh had done, and all the harm he wished to do, she longed for him to hurt in turn.

Aye then, she'd best be honest about it: for the first time ever in her life she had entered the sacred circle wishing to do harm.

The desire, opposed to everything she knew about white magic, nevertheless possessed her, a direct opposite to how she always sought to live her life—and gloriously seductive.

She bowed her head beneath the terrifying weight of it and whispered, "Help me."

"Annie."

Her mother's voice. Shock raced through her like a drench of cold water, and she raised her head; her eyes flew open.

Her mother sat across from her, inside the circle of light, eyes steady and hands folded.

Annie gasped. To be sure, she'd often felt her mother's presence since her death, had caught hints of her laughter or her words on the wind. Morag MacCallum existed in every part of Annie's life. And Annie had encountered her in dreams.

But this was no dream; now she came in truth, looking just as she had before she died, her black hair, well streaked with white, confined in a braid down her back. Quick, clever features too sharp to be considered bonny yet holding a rare beauty. Bright hazel eyes that brimmed with wisdom. Relief and wonder kicked through Annie powerfully.

"Mother."

"Child."

"How is it you are here?"

"Your need has brought me. I come in love and warning."

Sol flapped his wings violently and arose from his perch. Both women watched as he circled the room, the air from his wings making the candles flicker. He flew through Morag's image and fluttered out the window.

"All my protectors have abandoned me," Annie said wryly and not without bitterness. "Uncle Dennis, you—now even Sol."

"Sol has but gone to watch the road. He will warn us if anyone approaches." Morag's eyebrow quirked even as it had in life. "And I am here, am I not? Do you call that abandonment?"

Annie struggled for breath. "How long can you stay?" She wanted her mother back forever. "It is so hard struggling on wi'out you."

Morag smiled. "I am always here, child. But 'tis time for you to walk your own path. Nothing stays the same; the seasons follow each other, and day follows night. So you shall take up your power and follow me."

"Mother, everything I ha' attempted has crashed down around me. Tell me what I am to do about Ned Randleigh—about Tam."

"Use the strength that lies within you. Embrace it, live it. Trust it."

"The strength?" Annie felt very little strength at the moment. "You mean, the magic? Mother, do you speak of the power that always awaits beyond the light, the dark half of what you have taught me to use? That which tempts me even now?"

"Daughter, is that the course you contemplate?"

"The power exists, I can feel it just beyond the barriers I have raised against it—those you taught me to erect." Annie licked her lips. "I need only stretch out my mind and seize it."

"Not your mind, Annie, but your soul. At present, your spirit remains untainted and burns with a pure flame. I can see that from where I stand. What have I taught you about dark power? It comes at a price and steals even as it gives."

"So does the 'mercy' Ned Randleigh offers," Annie said. "And I know no other way to defeat him. Mother, I have never in my life caused harm to anyone. But in my heart…in my heart I believe Ned Randleigh deserves to suffer harm."

"Unquestionably."

Annie leaned forward and eyed her mother earnestly. "So then perhaps I should seize this power and use it to serve him as he has coming."

For a moment, Morag did not respond. Her sharp features tightened, and her eyes filled with sorrow. All the candles in the room dimmed at once, as if a cold breath passed over them.

"So," Morag said then, "you would be the instrument for Ned Randleigh's just punishment, would you?"

"I would return to him what he has put out into the world—his cruelty to Kirstie, to Jockie, to Tam…" Her voice wavered when she spoke her husband's name. "To all the folk under his heel. What other choice have I?"

Morag answered the question with another. "Have I not bidden you to trust? Trust is no easy matter, not when trouble comes and fear takes up residence in the heart. But it maun follow true belief. Remember what I have taught you about the rules by which a white witch lives."

"Do no harm. And—and whatever we put out into the world will return to us, times three."

"Do you not believe this?"

"I do."

"Then, Daughter, have faith. As I ha' told you, *trust*."

"But I do no' see—"

"You do no' have to see. Faith does not require you seeing—only believing."

Tears flooded Annie's eyes. "Then I find that perhaps I do no' believe after all, no' the way I should. For when I think of Tam, doubt possesses my heart. It has been hard, Mother—so hard wi' you gone, a heavy load carrying what you bore so easily."

"Did you suppose it easy for me, after your father died? 'Twas a long walk, Daughter, down a narrow path alone. But, as you will find, there is strength won in each step. And you maun look on my passing as an opportunity."

"An opportunity!"

"Aye, for had I not moved on, you would have kept following me and would no' have needed to take those steps on your own. You would no' have gone to the hiring fair; you would never ha' met Tam Sutherland."

Annie closed her eyes on a rush of pain. "Mother…"

"Do you no' see, Annie, this is your time, and a privilege for you to find your way? It may no' be the same as my way, so stop wi' trying to be me. Be the woman you were born to become. And in doing that, Daughter, I bid you again, keep your heart pure. Do not succumb to the lure of the darkness."

Annie drew a breath. "But if I did use that power— Mother, tell me true; would I then be able to defeat Ned Randleigh? Could I free Tam?" For she cared much less about her own welfare than his.

"Perhaps so. But remember, the greatest threat Ned Randleigh represents is to your spirit."

Morag leaned forward, and Annie felt the merest brush of her mother's fingers on her brow. "Go with the light, Daughter," she whispered, and dissolved into the air.

Annie bowed her head and wept.

Chapter Twenty-Six

The lock on Tam's prison rattled, and the door creaked open abruptly. He struggled to his feet.

"Out," Ned Randlcigh said.

The man wore a sour expression and carried a firearm, which he waved in Tam's direction. In the hallway beyond lurked two of his henchmen, putting paid to any hope Tam might harbor for escape.

He hesitated a moment. "Where are you taking me?"

Randleigh's cold eyes swept over him. "Your wife has returned with the physician."

Tam's heart leaped, and he went forward willingly. The men bullied him down several corridors to what must be the parlor, a large room filled with gloomy morning light. Outside the tall windows it rained, a true Highland rain that sluiced down the glass panes and pounded the ground.

Tam barely noticed, for Annie stood clad all in her green cloak and dress, now darkened with wet, and the physician, Camden, beside her.

Yet another man was present as well, seated behind a broad table, a heavyset fellow wearing a deep frown.

"Tam." Annie started forward to him, her dark gaze touching him avidly. "Husband, how are you?"

To be certain, Tam scarcely knew; pain and anger—and the longing for her—had taken such a toll on him he barely recognized himself.

And Annie, his Annie, did not look well. Agony filled her eyes, her face white with strain, and she'd clearly been crying. He ached to take her in his arms.

Instead he asked, very low, "Who is that man?"

In a whisper, she replied, "The magistrate, Master Belfour. Not the man Randleigh expected. We ha' some hope…"

"Enough!" Randleigh declared. "Let Master Camden do his work. I would delay the magistrate no longer than necessary."

"I am eager to go nowhere in this downpour," said the heavyset man easily. "Please, Master Camden, take your time."

"Thank you, Master Belfour." The physician approached Tam and separated him from his guards the way a collie might nose a lamb from the flock. "Let us see how you are healing."

He examined Tam's swollen and splinted hand, and the stripe across his face, as well. His eyes, which measured Tam's general condition, contained a measure of compassion.

"Tell me, Master Sutherland, how have you been treated here in your imprisonment?"

Tam had to choke back his rage before he could speak. "Sir, the care you provided last time you were here is all I ha' seen."

"Have you been provided food and sufficient water? You appear to be deficient in both."

"One meal and one cup of water a day."

Randleigh blustered, "The man is a prisoner. I refuse to coddle him."

"Still," the magistrate said weightily, "there is a

moral principle here, surely. Tell me, Sutherland, how did you sustain those injuries?"

"Sir, as befits my hand, the original injury occurred last winter. In the time since I married my wife, it improved markedly. These recent injuries you see were inflicted by the factor, Ned Randleigh."

The magistrate lifted his brows. "How is that?"

Tam met Belfour's gaze levelly. "When I was taken into custody, Ned Randleigh crushed my hand beneath his boot, causing this injury you see."

Randleigh began to bristle, but the magistrate held up his hand, gaze never wavering from Tam's. "And that slash across your face?"

"A blow from Ned Randleigh also."

Belfour looked at the physician.

"Three broken fingers," Camden contributed, "and undoubted ligament damage. Only by a mercy did the blow to the face miss blinding him."

Belfour looked at Randleigh then. "What have you to say, sir, to these accusations?"

Randleigh blustered, "I am not on trial here. The man attacked me and had to be subdued. His hand may well have been injured in the struggle. The rest is all exaggeration."

Doggedly, Camden said, "The prisoner was then provided no care until his wife sent for me."

Belfour's frown deepened still further; he shifted uncomfortably in his chair. "Master Randleigh, I cannot think this proper handling of the situation. What have you to say?"

Randleigh drew himself up. "Master Belfour, it is much fuss about nothing. You and I both know these sorts of people are little better than animals—"

"So you would treat an animal thus, would you? Where is your moral sense?"

Annie exchanged a look with Tam, and he saw hope fill her eyes. Master Belfour, it seemed, was not in Ned Randleigh's pocket. Had they a chance after all?

"Sir," Randleigh said coldly, "Laird Ardaugh has laid upon me the charge of overseeing his estate. I will do whatever I must to protect his interests. It is not wise to allow these tenants any leeway, or they tend to take grievous advantage."

"This man took advantage of you, did he?" Belfour asked and ran his gaze up and down Tam. "It does not look it."

"He attacked me, his better," Randleigh snarled.

"Tell him why." Head high and black eyes snapping, Annie spoke for the first time.

"It does not matter why. He is a subordinate—"

"'Tis what it all comes to in your sight, is it no'?" Annie challenged. "You feel everyone on Laird Ardaugh's land is beneath you, and yours to abuse as you will."

"Abuse?" Belfour picked up on the word. "Master Randleigh, this woman appears to be educated and of good birth. Of what abuse does she accuse you?"

Randleigh, looking suddenly uncertain, shook his head.

Annie stepped toward the table, and appealed earnestly, "Master Belfour, if I may be permitted to speak?"

"I think you should."

"Our Laird Ardaugh MacCallum has been long away and left his factor to manage the estate. 'Tis a common enough practice these days in the Highlands, I ken. But Master Randleigh has held the threat of clearance over our heads these past two years. He collects the rents and, if a woman canno' pay, demands something other than coin."

Belfour started and flushed red. "What is this you say?"

Annie lifted her head and directed a measured look at Randleigh. "He bargains for the woman's favors, sir, in exchange for leave to stay in her home."

"An ugly assertion."

"It is, sir."

Belfour turned his eyes on Randleigh who, in contrast to the magistrate, stood white with anger. "What do you say to this charge?"

"Spiteful and unfounded! This woman is entirely unreliable, Master Belfour, and would say anything in order to win her husband free. Why, you have no idea what she is or her standing in the district. You cannot expect truth from her; she is the local witch!"

Annie flinched visibly at the word; Tam stepped forward to her side protectively.

"That is a lie," he told Belfour. "My wife has some skill at healing—'tis what caused the improvement to my hand. But Randleigh has no call to go hurling such an accusation."

"She wreaks spells and distributes potions," Randleigh snapped in a vicious tone. "What else would you call her?"

"Compassionate," Tam returned swiftly. "A quality wi' which you ha' no acquaintance."

Annie lifted her head still higher. "If I be a witch, Master Randleigh, why did you threaten me and press so hard, before my marriage, for favors I was unwilling to give? This," she added to Belfour, "he should be afraid to do, did I possess dark powers."

Belfour returned his stare to Randleigh. "Is this true? Did you press this woman as she says?"

"Absolutely not. There is no proof. And it has no bearing on the matter at hand."

"Och, but I think it does," Tam said, "for you claim I attacked you. I was in fact attempting to protect another such woman, Master Belfour, and to get between the factor and her companion—a young man the factor had already thrashed within an inch o' his life and meant to harm again."

"Lies," Randleigh spat. "Will you believe such a ruffian as this? I say again, there is no proof."

"Oh," Annie said softly, "but there is."

She stepped to the door and pushed it open. Belfour cocked his head curiously as a low conversation took place. An instant later, Kirstie and Jockie stepped into the room.

Tam, staring in amazement, could not decide which of them looked more daunted. Jockie came with his customary hesitant gait and the livid welts still clearly visible on his face. Kirstie, hands folded, shot a wild look at Belfour and the physician before fixing her stare on Ned Randleigh and shrinking toward Jockie's side.

To Tam's surprise, Jockie reached out and seized her hand.

"What is this?" Belfour asked.

"This woman is Kirstie MacLachlan, a tenant living on her croft wi' but her aged grandmother. Master Randleigh forced her, just as I ha' said. The lad is my own farmhand, Jock, who tried to defend her when the factor returned for more. You can see how

Master Randleigh dealt wi' him."

Tam experienced a rush of combined hope and dismay. How courageous of these two to come here for his sake, and Annie's. Poor Kirstie, her cheeks flaming with embarrassment, could not meet the magistrate's gaze, but Jockie stared at Randleigh with unflagging hatred.

"An outrageous charge!" Randleigh declared swiftly. "And unfounded. The boy, as you can see, is a halfwit."

"He is not," Annie refuted. "He may have difficulty speaking, but his wits, Master Belfour, are as clear as yours or mine."

Belfour leaned forward and eyed Jockie with interest. "Young man—Jock, is it? What is the nature of your affliction?"

Jock considered the question and shrugged. His face twisted with effort as he said, "Do no' rightly ken, sir."

"The dolt cannot even speak," Randleigh decried. "Master Belfour, you cannot accept his testimony."

"I think I may," Belfour mused. "Do you, Jock, understand who I am? I serve here as magistrate and an authority for justice. Do you swear to speak true at peril of your soul?"

Jockie nodded.

"Who caused these wounds I see upon you?"

Jockie nodded at Ned Randleigh, the gesture rendering words unnecessary.

"For what reason?" Belfour persisted.

"Let me say for him." Clearly terrified, her voice shaking, Kirstie spoke up. "I was there." She turned her eyes, full of horror and dread, on Randleigh. "This man did come to my door one night and say he would toss both me and my grandmother from our home. Sir, my grandmother is ill, bedridden. I felt I had no choice but to pay the price he asked to let us stay."

"What price is this?" Belfour asked, even as Ned Randleigh bristled.

Kirstie bowed her head and began to weep.

"No matter," Belfour looked uncomfortable. "I believe I understand."

"Sir!" Randleigh barked. "This is a false accusation. The foolish cow lies in an effort to blacken my reputation."

"Why should she wish to blacken your reputation, Master Randleigh?"

"She is behind on her rent. I have been more than lenient."

"Have you?"

"Curious that," Tam spoke, "how he only shows such leniency to women living on their own."

"Kirstie MacLachlan tells the truth," Annie stated starkly. "She came to me the next day because he used her so harshly—"

Jockie mewled with vehemence.

"That is when Jockie—my farmhand—went to stay wi' her," Annie continued, "in an effort to protect her should the factor return."

"Which he did more than once," Tam took it up. "On the second occasion, I arrived and attempted to get between them. Randleigh then ordered his men to seize me."

"Lies!" Randleigh howled. "Master Belfour, whom will you believe—this lot of ruffians, or me?"

All eyes moved to Belfour, including those of

Camden, who looked particularly interested.

"Why would Mistress Kirstie and young Jock lie?" Belfour asked Randleigh.

"These peasants are wont to close ranks, sir, as you would know if you were in my position. They are deceitful and lie for one another like breathing."

"Then tell me, Master Randleigh, who or what inflicted the injuries I see upon young Jock, here?"

"How can I say if I was not there? All I know is this man, Tam Sutherland, attacked me. My own men will attest to that. You must find him dangerous and at the very least assign a sentence of deportation."

"So that you may then get at my wife?" Tam challenged. "When she, like Kirstie, is alone and defenseless?"

"That witch, defenseless?" Randleigh sneered. "She should be put on trial for the use of dark arts."

"Enough!" Belfour slapped the table with his palm. "Master Randleigh, you say I must find this man, Tam Sutherland, dangerous. Do you think to tell me my duty?"

"No, sir."

"No. Young woman…" Belfour turned to Kirstie and asked not unkindly, "do you swear on your immortal soul that what you have told me here today is truth?"

Kirstie, still in tears and clutching Jockie's hand, gulped and nodded.

"Then"—Belfour paused weightily—"I have no proof otherwise. Just as I have no proof Tam Sutherland attacked Ned Randleigh in anything but self-defense or that Master Randleigh broke Sutherland's hand. I find, Ned Randleigh, you have no cause, either, to hold him.

He must be released."

Annie gasped, and her face lit with joy. But Randleigh glowered.

"This is an outrage. Master Mowatt, the magistrate assigned to this district, would not—"

Swiftly Belfour interrupted, "Ah, but Master Mowatt is suffering from a severe case of gout and cannot travel. Hence I have been appointed to cover for him. Would you, sir, question my fitness?"

Clearly Randleigh did, but he muttered, "No, sir."

"Then let this matter be done and over. I order the release of Tam Sutherland." He turned to Kirstie. "You, young woman, have shown great courage in coming forward."

Jockie put his arm around the shaking girl.

Belfour returned his gaze to Ned Randleigh. "Let me hear no more of such incidents, sir, on your patch."

"Thank you, Master Belfour." Annie stepped past Randleigh and took Tam's good hand.

As she did, Tam heard Randleigh say to her in a dangerous undertone, "Well played, mistress. But you shall most certainly pay for this."

Chapter Twenty-Seven

Night had come; the rain still fell outside, as it had all through their journey home and during the celebratory meal Sonsie prepared after. Now night settled softly around the stone cottage. Jock and Kirstie had gone home, Kirstie citing duty to her grandmother. The animals all tended, Sonsie had cleared the dishes and climbed to her bed in the loft. At long last, Tam and his wife were alone.

Annie barred the door and turned to Tam softly, a host of emotions in her eyes. Hunger rose within him, hard and fierce, that had little to do with food. Suddenly the pain and grief he'd harbored these past days eased, leaving but one desire: to take her in his arms, taste her lips, and experience again the sense of completeness that only seemed to find him in her company.

She reached for him blindly, and he felt her tremble. "Och, how I feared for you," she said.

He drew her closer. "And I for you."

"And I missed you."

"Did you, so?" He should not question it. Only look what she'd gone through to succor him and pry him loose from Randleigh's hold. Yet the doubts the factor planted in his mind while yet she was away had put down barbed roots and burrowed deep.

"Surely you do no' doubt me?" She leaned up and kissed him tenderly. Their lips melded together, and desire leaped bright as fire. Annie sagged against him.

Into his mouth she gasped, "Tam, please."

He caught her face between his hands, the one splinted and curled against her cheek, and gazed into her eyes. "Annie, are you sure 'tis me you want?"

"Whom else?"

"A hundred other men, a thousand better suited to you, and more deserving. Yon Randleigh is right in what he says about me."

"I care naught for Ned Randleigh. Shall I prove it to you?" She kissed his lips once more before moving on to his chin, his throat, and the skin at the open neck of his shirt. Her nimble fingers went to work on the buttons of the garment.

"Annie, nay." He drew away from her. "I am filthy from my confinement."

"Then let me wash you, tend you as I ha' ached to do." Her gaze met his, unstinting and honest, hiding nothing. "You just stand there," she bade and bustled off to pour hot water into a basin. When she came back with a soft cloth and soap, she set the basin at his feet.

"Annie, you need not tend me."

"I want to." Gently she stripped off his shirt, easing it over his bad hand. She began to wash him with a tenderness that stopped Tam's throat, stroked his shoulders, arms and chest. When she sponged his injured hand she once more lifted it to her lips and blessed it with a kiss.

She reached next for the laces on his trousers. His eyes, soothed more than half shut, flew open.

"Annie…"

"Hush. Will you deny me the very pleasure I ha' craved?"

Tam exhaled.

Gently yet she stripped the trousers from him and without hesitation the trews beneath.

"Annie, wife—"

"Hush," she bade again. Tam began to tremble.

"Annie," he said for the third time.

She shed the cloth and dropped to her knees, cupping him in her hands. He felt her tongue caress him in a soft, lingering stroke an instant before she took him into her mouth.

The sweetness of it, tangled so closely with desire, nearly took Tam down where he stood. But he could not fall, not while Annie worshipped him with such pure devotion. Instead he buried his fingers—good and bad alike—in the glossy wealth of her hair and stood like a king while she devoured him, knowing no man could be higher than he, so favored by the wee magical crow, Annie.

Enchantment seemed to flow from her touch, inflaming Tam and sweeping away every doubt. Wracking desire coiled and flared inside him, and all too soon he gave himself up to her completely, erupting in wave after wave of scorching pleasure.

Avidly she accepted what he bestowed, linked with him flesh to flesh and soul to soul.

"Lass, lass, lass…" He breathed the words in humble gratification and lifted her up into his arms, where he strained her against him so tightly they might as well be one. He ached to tell her how he loved her but had no words. Instead he swept her up and carried her to the bed. "Sweet lass, you ha' made me feel the finest man alive."

"So you are, to me." She ran her hands over his

chest, tracing the muscles there and tangling with the hair. "Do you no' ken how it delights me to touch you?"

Tam could tell.

"I ached so terribly when you were apart from me."

He whispered, "Then let me ease that ache."

Her dark eyes followed his every movement as he began to remove her clothes. Curious, how clearly he could feel her emotions—almost as if they were his own, as if her pleasure was also his and they did indeed share one flesh. Man and wife.

Annie, his wife.

He told her huskily, "I want to taste you— everywhere. Will you let me worship you even as you did me?"

She lay back on the bed with a sigh, obedient as a child, a wordless invitation. Tam saw nothing childlike, though, in the way she looked at him or how she visibly took flame when he uncovered her breasts. Her nipples stood in stiff peaks that wooed his fingers, and he reared up for her as hard as if she had not already eased him.

He knew what he wanted—what she wanted—but he took a moment to admire her and implant the image she made in his mind. For he had learned one thing in life: things treasured must be remembered, lest they be snatched away never to come again.

And aye, what a picture she made pinned against the sheets, spread for him like a willing sacrifice—arms thrown wide, legs flung apart, hair fanned out around her, and her gaze hanging on his as if he breathed for her. If he could not tell her of his love in words, he would show her here, now, this night.

"Annie," he murmured, and bent his head.

This must be what she meant, he thought a bit wildly, when she said what a person put out into the world came back times three, for he'd meant only to provide her pleasure, yet a storm of ecstasy found him. The intimacy of kissing her in the most private of places, of entering her with his tongue and claiming the hot core of her womanhood engulfed him in a storm that mingled exultation with tenderness.

And she? He felt her pleasure spear through her with every movement of his lips as she arched herself into him, an act of total offering. And he experienced the fullness of her wracking pleasure when she came apart in his hands.

"Tam!" Fiercely, she drew him up into her arms even while she still rode the crest of her passion, held him so tight they might again be of one flesh. He breathed into her neck, and she clasped him as if she might never let him go.

Still hard, he nestled himself between her thighs. As soon as she felt him there she drew his head up and gazed into his eyes.

"Tam, please."

He made love to her slowly, luxuriantly, and when their joining became complete he supposed his heart might burst. They lay as one, breathless, and he groped for words to tell her what she meant to him.

But she spoke first, pressing wet kisses to his cheek. "Promise me something."

"Anything."

"Say you will never leave me. For I think I could bear aught else before losing you for any reason."

"I will never, never leave you, Annie Sutherland,"

he vowed readily.

Pray he could keep the promise.

Chapter Twenty-Eight

"Mistress?"

Annie looked up when she heard Jockie's voice and found him hovering in her doorway outlined in morning sunlight.

Four days had passed since Tam's release, since the night they had made such consuming—and binding—love. They'd lain together so each night since, and the feelings she now harbored for her husband terrified her. How dangerous to love and need another person so much! How helpless she was to resist.

Still she had not found words to tell Tam what he meant to her—she doubted such words existed. Yet she had only to look at him, catch a hint of desire in his clear, gray eyes, watch him at work, or receive his smile to feel like a woman reborn, just as if her world had stopped in his arms and begun turning anew.

And it seemed she saw everyone else anew, as well. Jock, for instance, surely held himself with more confidence, his hunch less pronounced and his pale blue gaze clear when it met hers.

"Good morn to you, Jockie. Is all well at Kirstie's place?"

He nodded, and a curious smile twitched his lips, as if he could not help but respond to the sound of Kirstie's name.

Annie knew how he felt.

"Mistress, I ha' come about you."

Even after living so long with Jockie, Annie had to listen hard in order to glean the words from his speech.

"Oh?" She straightened from the table where she'd been sorting herbs. Tomorrow being market day, she expected a large number of visitors.

"Aye."

"Well, come awa' in. You are no stranger here. Will you take a bit of breakfast?"

He shook his head but shuffled in and shut the door behind him.

"How are Kirstie and her grandmother?"

"T'auld woman is dyin'." Jockie spat the words out with determination.

"Eh?" Startled, Annie gazed at him. She knew Kirstie's grandmother for a stubborn creature set on staying in her home and her bed, content to have others wait upon her—perhaps far too ornery to die.

But Jockie nodded insistently. "She does no' like that Kirstie has taken up wi' me and says she will p-perish before she accepts it."

"I see. And," Annie asked frankly, "has Kirstie taken up wi' you, then?"

"Aye." Jockie lifted his head proudly. "We are friends. And I ha' spent each night in her bed."

Annie tried to conceal her shock. Why should Jockie, with his warm, generous heart, not find a measure of happiness even as she, Annie, did with Tam? And bless Kirstie for seeing past the cage in which the lad was trapped to the shining soul beneath.

Softly she said, "I am that happy for you."

"When t'auld woman dies, we mean to leave here."

194

"Leave?"

"Go across the water to Canada."

Dismay speared through Annie in the wake of the happiness. She sank into a seat at the table. And so was she to lose Jockie from her life? Aye, and had she not just been thinking about how the circle now spun in a new direction? Jock had a right to his happiness if he could seize it.

"Och, and I will miss you." Tears filled Annie's eyes.

Jockie nodded somberly. "You should think o' leaving, too—you and your man."

Her man. Was Tam that? Och, aye, if she had aught to say about it.

But she shook her head. "I canno' leave here, Jock. I ha' too many people depending on me."

"Aye, but Kirstie was all about t'district these last days, selling her wares." Kirstie made soaps and sold them to raise a few extra pennies. "She has heard naught but talk o' you."

"Me?"

"'Tis why I came—to warn you, just." Jockie's pale eyes flooded with dismay. "Everywhere she went, she heard the same: someone is goin' about spreadin' word you be a witch."

"What?" Annie stiffened.

Jockie gazed at her in dismay. "'Tis a gey dangerous thing, mistress."

Alarm speared through Annie, and dread followed after. *Not that.* True, the danger had always lurked for her and her mother both, but they had been so careful to avoid any taint of darkness.

"No need," she muttered, "to ask who has started

such talk." She stumbled to her feet. "Ned Randleigh means to destroy me."

"Aye—because you ha' defied him. We all have. But he kens fine harming you will hurt us most."

Annie stared at the lad, feeling as if the floor fell away beneath her feet.

"Och, Jockie," she whispered, "what am I to do?"

"Leave this place e'en as we mean to do."

Leave here? For the first time Annie truly considered it. But the place was part of her, in her blood and in her bone. Should she allow one evil man to chase her from it?

Better, far better, to destroy the threat Ned Randleigh represented.

****

"How does that feel?"

Tam groaned in appreciation as Annie stroked the palm of his injured hand. He lay on his back in the big bed, completely sated and more than half drunk with pleasure. Annie had just loved him right well, and now he could feel healing flowing from her gentle fingers into his knitting bones.

Those fingers—as well as her soft lips—had been all over him, elevating him once more to the status of a king. His contentment would be complete did he not harbor the nagging conviction that something bothered her—something she sought to hide from him.

He turned on his side and sought her face in the light from the dying fire. The animals lay everywhere around them, and Sol sat on his perch, but Tam had got used to that. Just as he'd grown used to Annie's presence in his life, a subtle music he now needed like breath.

He let his eyes caress the smooth line of her shoulder, breast, and hip, and touch the tangled wealth of glossy hair spread on her pillow.

"Annie, wife, you are so bonny."

Her fingers stilled on his hand; he heard her breath catch.

"I am that glad you think so, husband."

"How could I think aught else?" He let the fingers of his good hand trace the graceful line his eyes had followed, marveling at her perfection. Whatever came to him in the future, at least he'd had these precious days and nights with her. Nothing could take that from him.

His hand found the soft weight of her breast and she leaned in to kiss him. When the sweet exchange ended, she whispered, "Will you love me again, Tam Sutherland?"

"You ken fine I will. But first I would ha' you tell me what troubles you."

She stiffened where she lay. "Me? Naught."

"Annie, I hoped we would keep no secrets from one another." There certainly seemed room for none when they clove together so completely and made one flesh. "Yet you are keeping somewhat from me."

She gave a sigh. "Have you spoken wi' Jockie?"

"Jock? Nay, why?"

"He came to see me this morning. To warn me. It seems Ned Randleigh is going about the district talking up the fact that I am—a witch."

She spoke the word barely above a whisper, as if she feared loosing it into the room. Aye, and it felt like a demon let out of a cage, in this peaceful place—abroad to do mischief and damage.

Tam tensed in response.

"But…" Dismay nearly stopped his throat. "No one will heed aught he says of you. They know what he is—and what you are, for that. You do good for everyone you touch."

"I have tried so hard to continue my mother's work, to carry on as she would ha' done. But, Tam, it comes to me now—perhaps that is no' enough. Perhaps I need to act in my own right, seize my own power."

Tam frowned, not certain he understood. "Eh?"

"I canno' live her life over again. I maun live mine here wi' you and out there facing Randleigh." She shivered. "I am ashamed to say the prospect frightens me."

"I do no' want for you to be frightened. How can I help?" The best person he'd ever known, Annie deserved whatever he could do in her defense.

But she shook her head. "I do no' think you can. My mother says—"

"Your mother!"

"She spoke to me, advised me."

Now Tam fell silent, wondering.

Annie went on, "I ha' choices before me. Decisions only I can make that will determine the pattern of my life."

Aye, and did those choices include deciding whether to keep him, Tam, with her? For he knew very well their marriage had started out a lie, and even though she'd taken him to her bed and he brought her pleasure, she might at any time change her mind about him, move on with her magical life and leave him behind.

If she did not destroy herself first.

He seized her wrist. "List to me, Annie. You maun be careful. The folk round here, aye, will take your part against Ned Randleigh, but that may no' keep him from plotting against you. Bad enough you curried his anger by winning me free—"

"No fault to you, in that. The trouble stems all from him; he is like a spider spinning a trap and always, I fear, a few steps ahead of me." She seemed to muse, "Even our marriage did not placate him as I ha' hoped."

Tam experienced a pain to his heart, as if thumped hard in the chest. Did his Annie, his beautiful Wee Crow, rue their joining after all?

"'Tis up to me," she whispered, "to stand on my own, be my own woman, and fight this battle."

Tam prayed she would continue wanting him to stand at her side.

Chapter Twenty-Nine

"Witch."

The whispered word flew at Annie like a flung stone, and not the first time she'd heard it this morning. Market day, and she had waited long for the women to begin streaming to her door as they always did. But her door, standing open to the pale sunshine, remained empty—no visitors on market day for the first time in her memory. Even as a young lass she had seen the women coming to her mother for charms, advice, and remedies.

The folk round here will take your part, Tam had said, and aye, she'd believed that. She'd not doubted the love and caring she put out into the world would come back to her tripled. But now she began to think again.

Was it possible her friends' and neighbors' fear of the factor outweighed even their appreciation for her past kindness?

It had taken a wealth of talking and persuasion for her to convince Tam she should go to the market when no one came to her—and then he insisted on accompanying her, a silent presence at her side. She wore her green cloak, the strength of it surrounding her like her mother's arms, but that did no good. For it seemed she—and Tam with her—had ceased to exist.

Folk they met on the road purported not to see

them. If she passed someone at his gate, he stared at the horizon. When she spoke a greeting, the recipient proved deaf. The most she won from anyone was a brief glance before his or her eyes fled.

Aye, and Jockie had tried to warn her of what Ned Randleigh intended. She had not dreamed, though, the factor could spread his poison so swiftly. Yet he—and the men with him—did the job of instilling fear and hate all too well.

For when Annie and Tam reached the market, they found Randleigh's men there before them, everywhere among the barrows and stalls, speaking the dreaded word and intimidating any who might otherwise speak in Annie's defense. Her anger grew as she went, tinged with more than a bit of fear every time one of Randleigh's henchmen repeated the word, like a curse.

"Witch." Unleashed like a weapon while she inspected Agnes MacEwan's jars of rowan jam. Agnes—whom Annie had cured of the ague just last winter—shrank from her, one eye on the men who circulated through the crowd, and out of pity for her Annie drew Tam on.

"Witch." Again, several moments later when she paused to inspect some potatoes for sale. She looked up to encounter the gaze of the old man standing behind the potatoes. Looking apologetic, he quickly avoided her eyes. Would no one here speak up for her? Did no one have the courage to defy Ned Randleigh?

"Enough of this," Tam breathed in her ear. "Come awa' home."

But she drew her arm from his grip, turned about, and gazed wildly at the faces that surrounded her. Several women of her acquaintance stood nearby—all steadfastly avoiding her gaze. Indeed, the only ones who would look at her directly were Randleigh's men, surely more in number than they had been before, and they kept her under close observation.

Annie focused on the nearest woman. "Good morn, Molly. How is your wee bairn doing now?" The child had greeted nonstop with colic until Annie prepared a syrup of fennel to ease him.

Molly's face tightened, and she edged away into the crowd.

"And you, Mairi—how is that sore on your husband's leg?" Mairi and her husband, an older couple, worked their croft alone. He had cut his leg on a scythe several weeks ago and, it having taken poison, Mairi came to Annie for a salve.

Now the old woman's eyes filled with tears and she looked in the other direction.

Hurt and hopelessness arose together in Annie's breast. Tam was right; she should go home, try to make sense of this betrayal.

Stubbornness made her move on instead, the conviction she could find at least one person willing to stand up for her, to defy Randleigh's watchful men. Yet the silence only seemed to grow around them as they went, until it filled the normally bustling market.

The unnatural quiet made it even more shocking when there came a sudden clatter of hooves on the cobbles, and a voice rang out.

"Mistress Sutherland!"

Annie and Tam both swung to see the crowd part like the Red Sea, admitting Ned Randleigh on his big black horse. Fear, cold and primal, slithered down Annie's spine, for danger preceded the factor like a cold wind. But how could he harm her here among all these folk, and with Tam at her side?

And if she now endangered Tam, the man she loved more than her own life? Och, why had she insisted on coming? They should have stayed safe at home. If any place was safe for her now…

She could feel the tension run up Tam's arm and through her own body. What if he acted to defend her, and the bones in his poor hand barely set? She'd counted no less than half a score of Randleigh's men planted in this crowd. Tam, for all his courage, would not stand a chance.

She wished she could wrap her love around him, keep a lid on his anger, wished with sudden passion she could cast a spell on Ned Randleigh and remove him like a blight.

The factor wore his broad, black hat on his head and an ugly, intent look on his face. His cold eyes fixed on Annie as if he saw nothing else, not even the man at her side. Folk shrank back from him in a widening circle, like ripples spreading out from a rock tossed in water.

He addressed Annie in a harsh voice that rang through the market. "What is in your pouch?"

"Eh?" The question, the last Annie had expected, shook her. "I beg your pardon?"

"Your pouch, woman." Randleigh nodded at the leather sack Annie wore as always, fastened to her belt.

Annie's fingers fluttered to it, even as she tried to discern her level of danger. Beside her, Tam remained stiff and silent.

"Come, woman. You can no longer hide what you have been about all this while, with your cures and potions. The truth has come home to you, and you stand accused of a grievous crime: witchcraft!"

A ripple of horror ran through the listening crowd. Annie felt it travel straight to her heart and tear through Tam also. For an instant, her knees weakened. Nay, not that! Her mother had always been so careful to keep any such charge from their door. Now, left on her own, Annie had failed—failed in all things.

"Lies!" Tam barked, sounding very like Ruff. "How dare you accuse a good woman o' such a thing?"

"Good woman?" Randleigh switched his narrowed gaze to Tam, acknowledging him for the first time. "Does a good woman take payment from folk for magical remedies? Does she surround herself with a host of familiars? Does she take strays—including human strays—to serve as her minions? Does the spirit of her uncle, in owl form, haunt her house?"

The crowd had now gone so quiet Annie could hear a bairn wail.

She huffed out a breath, and Tam spoke again. "You twist the truth, factor!"

"We shall have the truth here and now," Randleigh declared. "Woman, I ask you again, what is in your pouch?"

"Herbs."

"Herbs!" Randleigh repeated victoriously. "Used for casting spells? Answer truthfully and it will go easier with you."

"Nay, I cast no spells," Annie denied. "I use these only for making cures—"

"Potions, then." Randleigh glared at the hushed crowd. "You have all heard her admit her guilt." He said to his men. "Seize her. And if her *husband* gets in the way, beat him down."

"Nay!" Annie spread her arms and made a barrier of her body. "You will not hurt him again!"

Tam, though, pushed her aside and shouted, "She has done no harm!"

"No harm—the cry of every witch ever burned at the stake," Randleigh declared.

Burned? Heat suffused Annie where chill had held her. Surely—surely someone would speak up for her? Surely the crowd as one would intervene, keep Randleigh's men from hurting Tam—her Tam!—and take her part.

Yet no one so much as moved as Randleigh's men closed in from everywhere in the crowd, no one but Tam, who snarled and made as if to leap forward. Her fear for him flared much brighter than any she felt for herself. She rounded on him and said, "Nay, Tam—it is no use. And I can face anything rather than see you hurt. Or killed." She whispered to him, "He is just looking for an excuse to kill you."

The rage in Tam's gray eyes terrified her almost more than her own plight. She leaned in and kissed him fiercely, an effort to forestall the words she could see hovering on his lips.

As if in response to the gesture, Randleigh snarled, "Hold him—and take her."

No fewer than four men laid hold of Tam and wrested him from Annie. He bucked and fought even as she willed him to stillness, and his gaze reached for hers.

"Where are you taking her? Where—"

"She will have her case heard. All shall be done properly and fairly. This very day I will send for the priest."

Father Alban, Annie thought desperately—aye, surely he would take her part. She calmed slightly, seeing that Tam had stilled in his captors' hands.

"Take care of Sonsie and the animals—" she called to him even as Randleigh's men drew her away. And may all the powers take pity on her plight.

Chapter Thirty

"What do you want of me? You ken fine this charge you ha' made against me is false. You canno' put me on trial for—for witchcraft."

Annie forced herself to speak the dreaded word and swayed where she stood. She had been standing here ever since they arrived at the laird's house, in front of the same table where Tam had stood before. Emotions ravaged her relentlessly all the while—terror, uncertainty, and this terrible dread—but Randleigh said little. He merely sat writing on some papers while Annie's knees grew weak and she feared more than once she would fall.

She could not so disgrace herself, though, in front of this man. Ned Randleigh wanted to break her—he had set her prey to her fears so he could watch her crumble. Of that she had no doubt.

Somehow, despite her trembling legs and soured stomach, she lifted her chin. "I am no witch."

"Are you not?" he spoke at last and looked up to fix her with his cold stare. He laid his pen aside and got to his feet.

All at once Annie rued the fact that she had his attention and that they were the two of them alone in the chamber. She had no doubt his men stood guard outside the door, but no one could see what he might do to her here.

He had arranged things so he could be alone with her. By the powers, she'd no need to ask what he wanted. She knew; she had always known.

Outside the parlor window, a crow cawed, the cry sharp and raucous. Ignoring the sound, Randleigh approached her.

"But mistress, I have evidence which I've collected over some time to say you have been practicing the dark arts."

"What evidence?"

"The contents of your pouch, for one thing." He had taken it from her when they arrived, wrested it away without mercy. "Herbs for casting spells."

"They are nothing of the kind. Merely for simples…"

"Simples." He pronounced it like a curse. "But another word for potions, that. And I am certain we will find far more such incriminating material when we search your house."

New horror speared through Annie. "You have no call to go there! No right."

"As your landlord's agent, I have every right. And if those in residence resist me, they may be dealt with, men and dogs alike."

Tam. And her beloved Ruff and sweet, sweet Ella—Sonsie, if she sought to protect them. And she would.

Annie's traitorous legs did give way then. She began to sink, but Randleigh seized her arm and hauled her up again, his touch relentless.

Coldly he accused, "You are a witch, and your mother before you. I have countless witnesses who stand ready to speak out against both her and you. No one would blame me for stamping out an evil that has infested this little pocket of the Highlands so long."

"Evil?" Incredulous, Annie stared at him, even as she shrank from his touch. "'Tis what you are, accusing me just so you might ha' your way. Aye, I ken what you are about, and what you desire."

He leaned closer so his breath gusted across her cheek and assaulted her senses. "Then give it to me."

Defiant, Annie glared into his eyes. "That which you would take belongs to my husband alone."

"Your husband? That dirty crofter? He is barely fit to lick your boots. Why would you offer such a privilege to him when you knew I wanted it?" His eyes narrowed. "Or is that why? Is this some game you play with the farmer, taunting me?"

"No game." Could he not feel her terror? Swaying in his grasp, she spoke the words she'd never been able to gift Tam. "I love him."

Randleigh bared his teeth in a laugh. "Now, that I will never believe. You, love that worthless outcast? And you an educated woman. Do not insult my intelligence."

"For mercy's sake, would you have me against my will?"

"I will take you any way I can get you, mistress." His gaze moved from her hair and down her face to her throat and bosom dispassionately. "A curious thing—you are not even that beautiful, one feature taken after the other. Yet all together you are the most alluring woman I have ever seen. I must have you at any cost. If that is not magic—black magic—tell me what is."

"I ha' never practiced black magic." But she wanted to now, at this moment. She wished to strike this man down where he stood, unleash a power that might destroy him.

Outside the window the crow cawed again.

"Yes? And do you wager anyone will believe that? Will you bet your life?"

Annie shrank in his grasp.

"Your death will be painful," he grunted. "There will be torture first—I can promise you that. I will also make sure all those you care for are destroyed before you—those beasts you value so highly, along with that ugly little maid and your deformed servant. A favor to the world, that. And your husband—ah, what shall I do to him? That depends on the choices you make."

"You are vile!" Annie spat.

Something dark flickered in his eyes. "That opinion will change when you feel me—a real man— between your legs, witch. You will scream my name, and not in fear."

"If you truly believe me a witch, why are you no' afraid of me?"

"Even a witch can be forced to obey if a man is strong enough, and uses the right discipline. Like all women, you are meant for but one purpose." His grip on her arm tightened still more cruelly. "You can prevent these ills from befalling your beasts and servants. Only come to the laird's bedchamber with me now, and I will contrive a way to find you innocent."

"The laird's bedchamber?" Annie faltered.

Randleigh tossed his head. "I am laird here, as good as. I have all his power, and everyone must heed me. Why should I not take you in his bed? Over and over again."

"You do no' want me this way, under duress."

"I have said I want you any way I can get you, preferably naked, with that glorious hair loosed all around you." He flicked her with another glance, up and down. "But I need not force you; you will give me consent."

"I will no' bow to your demands, I would no' be so foolish."

"Shall I then send my men to your house with orders to clear out and slay all the creatures there—the cats, the fox, those vicious dogs, and the owl—all witch's familiars?"

Annie's eyes widened in horror. "Nay, please not that."

"You have the power to prevent it. You need but say the word."

But she belonged only and forever to Tam Sutherland.

The crow cawed a third time. Almost simultaneous with it there came a great pounding at the front door, audible even here in the quiet parlor.

Randleigh spat, "That, I do not doubt, will be your husband. Make up your mind swiftly, woman, or will you watch him pay the price?"

Chapter Thirty-One

"Give my wife over to me. She has done naught wrong." Tam spat the words while struggling to keep hold of his emotions, a near-impossible task.

He had borrowed the neighbor's horse—much faster than poor Old Rake—though the man, afraid of getting on the wrong side of the factor, refused to come with him or assist in any other way. A theme, that, among Annie's friends and neighbors who had failed to speak up for her at the market.

Now Tam stood in the entry hall, having forced his way, breathless as if he'd run the whole distance. Three men faced him—the same three who had taken him prisoner last time, and him unarmed save for his rage and determination.

All the way here his resolve had strengthened; he would not fail Annie as he had his parents, not even at pain of death. What was a man, after all, if he could not stand strong for the woman he adored?

And he did adore Annie with his every breath and each beat of his heart. His blood coursed through his veins for her sake.

Upon that thought, the door across from him—that which led to the parlor—opened. Ned Randleigh stood there with Annie caught hard in his hands.

Tam's heart leaped. He stepped forward, and all three of Randleigh's henchmen bristled.

"Annie! You are unharmed?"

She nodded stiffly, but he did not believe her. She looked terrified, her cheeks pale as milk, dark eyes glittering. Even from this distance he could see how her heartbeat stirred the green fabric of her bodice.

She spoke in a voice rough as a crow's squawk. "Go home, husband. Do no' make this worse than it has to be."

Worse? How could it be worse unless they tied her to a stake? And did she truly expect him to walk away from her? He would not, could not.

Randleigh said with a sneer, "Heed your wife's advice, Sutherland, while still you can claim your freedom. The priest has been summoned. This woman will stand trial and answer the charge of witchcraft leveled against her."

"Leveled by whom? You? She is no witch—you know that as well as I do."

"Think again. She has the necessaries needed to cast spells, both on her person and in her home."

"She has done naught but seek to aid her neighbors—"

"She has conjured defiance against me and thus against her laird. There must be a cleansing." Randleigh leaned toward Tam. "Fire. It is the means of choice."

If possible, Annie went still whiter and swayed as if only Randleigh's cruel grip kept her on her feet.

Harshly, Randleigh went on, "This woman and her mother before her have a long history in this district of practicing the dark arts. So far, out of mercy, I have turned a blind eye."

"Mercy!"

"Yet I can no longer do so. Get you back to the

dung heap from whence you came, Sutherland, unless you would die in her place."

Tam would, gladly. He knew he would trade all the days he had left on this earth to spare Annie one moment's pain. But he could not be foolish about it, spend his chances in anger and lose once again.

His gaze met Annie's, and it felt as if she spoke to him without words, inspiring a hundred images: her climbing the steps of the platform at the hiring fair; the compassion with which she tended those who came to her; the laughter in her face when she played with her dogs; the passion in her eyes when she reached for him, Tam—a host of gifts he'd not known he received, at the time.

How might he repay her for all of that?

"When will this trial begin?"

"As soon as the priest arrives. Until then, she will be held with great care and watched closely, insuring she can cast no spell and so free herself."

"Watched by whom?" Randleigh himself, Tam did not doubt.

"Leave that to me," Randleigh replied; horror and warning both clawed up through Tam's belly.

"When will Father Alban arrive?"

"It is not Father Alban. I have sent for a man of my acquaintance."

Another shred of Tam's hope died. He met Annie's terrified gaze again and read her thoughts there. Doomed. Even if the priest Randleigh summoned proved just and fair—a doubtful premise at best—he would likely not arrive before nightfall. That left the night stretching ahead, a night with Annie at this man's nonexistent mercy.

Tam lifted his chin. "I demand you let me speak with my wife alone."

"You demand?"

"As her husband, I ha' that right."

"You think I do not recognize your marriage as false? She barely knew you when she took you to her bed." Randleigh eyed Tam up and down. "Perhaps by now she has inducted you into her dark arts."

"If aught be a sham, 'tis your authority here. You use it like a weapon over these folk—well, no more! They shall rise up together and speak against you."

"Those craven wretches? You saw them at the market. Tell him, mistress. Tell your husband how many of your neighbors are likely to speak for you when the priest comes. Nary a one! If any does speak at her trial, Sutherland, it will be against her."

"Out of fear," Tam retorted. "If they want to stay in their homes, if they hope to keep their families safe, they will bow to you."

"Go home, Sutherland, and await the cleansing fire. Or better yet, leave the district and save yourself."

"I will no' leave here until I speak wi' my wife alone."

Randleigh opened his mouth to refuse, but Annie spoke before he could.

"Allow me to speak wi' my husband as he asks, so I may dismiss him from me—the better, Master Randleigh, to consider your offer."

Dismiss him? And what offer was this? Tam could just imagine.

Randleigh gave Annie a hard stare before he pushed her back toward the parlor. A crook of his head summoned Tam also.

"Ten minutes," he granted. "And yes, woman—if you know what is good for you, you will get rid of him."

****

The door shut behind Ned Randleigh, and Annie tumbled forward into Tam's arms.

Ah, by all that was sacred, she'd feared she might never touch him again. And she would trade more than her safety if it meant he might hold her, even for ten minutes.

She wanted to burrow into his warmth, into the illusion of safety he lent, yet there were so very many things that needed to be said. Randleigh was right— Annie needed to send Tam away from her, release him from whatever bonds of loyalty might tie him to her, and so allow him to save himself.

But she gazed up into his eyes and forgot everything save how she felt for him, a truth real and vital to her as her own breath. She'd not expressed those feelings in words, but perhaps he knew—he must have felt it in her caress, in the joy she took when they joined together. Aye, it must be so, for he reached at once for her lips as a drowning man might reach for air.

And Annie tasted so much in his kiss: strength, courage, devotion, and one thing more.

She wanted to linger there, pass forever in the completeness of his embrace with his tongue stroking hers. But she fought her way up, caught his face between her hands and gazed once more into his eyes.

"Tam. He is right, I am undone. You maun go— save yoursel'."

"You think I would? Nay, lass—if you are here, I am here also, live or die. For I love you. *Love you.* Do you no' ken that?"

Annie's knees went weak and she closed her eyes for an instant on a wave of pure bliss. Only Tam's arms kept her upright. "And I love you, Tam Sutherland. I scarcely ken why it has taken me so long to tell you so." She gave a laugh that sounded more like a sob. "But I think I always loved you, from that first moment."

"Aye, when our eyes met in the crowd. And then you climbed onto that platform and said your piece, and I knew you for a madwoman, far too grand and wonderful for the likes o' me. But I knew I would do anything—aught at all—to stay by your side. I would yet."

"Fools that we were, not speaking the words to one another. And it takes this—" Her voice broke.

"List to me, Annie. There maun be a way to win you free."

"There is. He has named his price: me in his bed, and then he will find me innocent."

"You canno'—"

"Nay, not after lying wi' you." She kissed him again, fierce and hot. "I belong only to you, Tam— body and spirit. Yet he has told me he will harm all I hold dear unless I relent—you and Sonsie, each of my animals. That is why you maun leave me. Go back home, bundle them all up, and take them away somewhere he cannot find them. If I know they—and you—are safe, I can endure anything."

"Lass, lass—you ken what he did to Kirstie."

Annie did. She swallowed back her fear. "Aye, but it may no' come to that." She gazed deep into Tam's eyes. "Once I know all of you are safe, I can take another path."

"What path?"

She licked her lips. Even speaking it felt abhorrent. But she lowered her voice to a whisper and said, "There are dark forces upon which I might call."

Tam's eyes widened in dismay. "Nay. Nay, Annie lass! That goes against all you are. Do no' let him force you into being what he accuses."

"But I must defeat him, and I ha' no other weapon."

Desperately, Tam told her, "You ha' the light—that which I ha' felt dwells within you. Use that, Annie. So I do implore you."

"I ha' tried." Wildly, Annie shook her head. "But it has no' protected me, or those I love."

"Lass, what is it you say your mother taught? That which you put out into the world returns times three. You have shed so much light just in the time I ha' known you. You maun believe it will return to you now."

She kissed him again, a third blessing. "Gift me now my peace of mind, Tam. Go from me and let me know you, Sonsie, and Jockie are beyond his reach."

"You expect me to walk from here and abandon you? Fail you even as I failed my ma and da?"

"You can never fail me." Tears now fell freely from Annie's eyes. "Take with you from this terrible place my light and all my love. I entrust you with both. Keep them safe for me."

"Annie, I beg you—do no' take this path you contemplate. Do no' betray yourself."

"What other course have I?"

"Trust me," Tam replied. "And trust the light."

Chapter Thirty-Two

Folks still lingered at the market, gossiping about what had occurred and speculating over Annie's fate. They stirred with renewed interest when Tam arrived, and gathered around him in a knot.

He had already stopped at Kirstie's croft and sent Jockie over to help roust Sonsie and the animals and get them to safety. He did not know where they might go—surely Kirstie's would prove no safer than Annie's farm, but the lad seemed to grasp the peril and had gone at once.

Tam tried to imagine the scene—Sonsie no doubt frantic, Jockie leading Old Rake away at a hobbling gait. They would have to leave all Annie's herbs and simples—evidence for Randleigh to use against her—and naught to be done about it.

Now he faced the remnants of the crowd, Annie's friends and neighbors, and prayed the law of three might prove true.

"I come to you on behalf of my wife, Annie MacCallum Sutherland, who has been seized under the charge of witchcraft!"

His voice clove the air of the market and struck every tongue silent.

"Most of you know her far better than I—you ha' had that great privilege. For she is a fine lady with a kind and generous heart, the best I ha' ever met. I will warrant there is no' a one of you here she has no' helped some way. I say to you now, 'tis time for you to help her in return."

Those in the group stirred again and stole uneasy glances at one another. None spoke.

Tam began singling out those he knew. "You, Stephen. I ken for a fact she helped tend your new bairn, and your wife in such a bad way. And you, Rory MacBain—has she no' been treating your wife's aching joints?"

"Aye, well," MacBain spoke up, "I repaid that debt when I accompanied her to Edinburgh to see Laird Ardaugh."

A woman said, "Mistress Annie has been good to us, aye, and her mother before her. But I've no wish to get crosswise of the factor. He will surely clear us from our home if I do, and me wi' wee bairns to protect."

"And so, will you sell your soul to him? Deny your conscience?"

"Aye," called a man, "if I ha' to. Would you no' do the same, Sutherland?"

He would in an instant, for Annie's sake. But he called back, "List to me, I ha' been where you stand, up north. I was tossed from our home of generations." He held up his hand. "It cost me dear, and not only in what you see. But I learned from that. There comes a time when a man—or woman—needs to stand up against the injustice and fight back."

"Stand up?" cried yet another man. "And fight how? We are at the mercy of that bastard. The laird does no' care for us; your wife traveled all the way to see him, and it made no difference."

Another woman took it up. "'Tis the laird who has

set that terrible great beast upon us."

"So you will let Annie Sutherland die?" Tam could scarce believe it. "Let him torture her first, and subject her to what you women know right well? She who has ne'er done aught but shed goodness on you all?"

His listeners stirred still more uneasily; some hung their heads.

"If we go and speak for her," one fellow said, "he will mark us and we will be the next to feel his ire."

"Be a man, for God's sake!" Tam retorted, despair laying hold of his heart. "Or lie forever beneath the factor's heel."

A cold wind swept across the market. As if it broke some spell, the people there turned away and began to move off, some gathering their unsold wares. Stunned, Tam stood, desperate to hold them and not knowing how. He'd been so sure Annie's touted law would hold, that her goodness would come back to her.

But these folk avoided his eyes and went. At last only a handful of people remained—three women and two men who approached him.

"I am Archie MacFey," said one elderly fellow. "Your wife brought mine a great deal of comfort before she died. I would repay that. What can I do?"

"Have you a horse?" Tam asked, a faint spark of hope igniting within him. "Old Rake has come up lame, and I need someone to go to Oban to fetch Father Alban."

The man shook his head, but the other, who proved to be Rory MacBain, said, "I will go fetch the priest."

"Aye," Tam agreed, "the sooner the better. Father Alban will speak for her, but he canno' come soon enough."

Rory nodded and jogged off, leaving Tam with a poor army indeed—one old man and three women, one of whom stood weeping quietly.

"The rest of you, if you ha' the courage, come with me to the laird's house and speak up for her. He means to stand her before a magistrate, but 'twill no' be the same man who heard my case—he will make sure this time 'tis the fellow who is in his pocket."

That might take some time, but meanwhile to what would his Annie be subjected? He shuddered to think.

"I will go wi' you," said MacFey, but the women exchanged terrified glances.

I need an army to free her, Tam thought, and beseeched every power he—and Annie—knew. *Send me an army.*

****

It took Annie—shut away in the same strong room where Tam had been held—far too long to stop shaking. All her courage had drained away, and her hands, knees, and teeth shuddered uncontrollably. She sat on the floor, as there was no other place, and held herself tightly—since there was no one else to hold her. She reached for strength that seemed slow to come.

Instead, intense longing for Tam filled her heart, and horrifying thoughts crowded her mind. Would she see Tam again? Perhaps at her "trial," which would be nothing but a sham. She believed he would come to support her. But he would then have to witness her humiliation and pain.

She needed him now. She needed his warmth and wit and the strength upon which she'd come to rely. And aye, she did rely upon him more than ever she'd dreamed she could. How had that happened so quickly and completely?

He loved her. She had that one comfort to carry to her grave.

Aye, but what might come before her death terrified her. Torture, piercing, burning with irons, pain—she'd heard what happened in the past to those accused of witchcraft, most of them probably innocent women using their knowledge of the natural world to help others.

Like her.

She had never understood, while growing up, just how much Uncle Dennis's relationship with Laird Ardaugh protected her and her mother. The two men played chess or cards together; they exchanged books, and had long discussions about philosophy.

But Uncle Dennis had gone, and the laird, no longer in residence, would not see her. All her protectors had flown.

Save Tam. And what could he do for her, one man alone?

He loved her, she reminded herself yet again. And that must prove comfort enough, a great strength no matter what came.

She needed to save herself.

Yet Tam had begged her not to use the one weapon available to her. As had her mother, who now dwelt in the other world.

What to do?

She got to her feet and began pacing in the limited space even as her teeth continued to chatter. She knew how to reach for the darkness; it hid among the folds of the light with which she'd worked so long, its strong opposite, always waiting for her to choose it. The light, she knew, could accomplish wondrous things; the darkness must be every bit as powerful.

Could it defeat Randleigh? A whisper of knowledge told her so. And should he come to her in this barren place tonight, demand that which she'd granted only Tam Sutherland, she might not be able to keep herself from using it.

That frightened her most of all, for in her heart she did not want to be that which Randleigh branded her.

"Help me," she breathed and heard a flutter at the window that spun her around.

Very nearly dark—she could see little but a movement there. She narrowed her eyes, and the bird gave a raucous cry, loud in the small room. A crow!

Wee Crow. She heard her uncle's voice again, repeating what Tam had said.

Trust.

"Please, Uncle. Do not leave me here alone. And do not let Tam endanger himself."

Better she should die in agony than allow Ned Randleigh to take out his ire upon Tam.

As if in answer, the bird dropped down into the room.

Chapter Thirty-Three

"What do you mean to do, just?" Aged Archie MacFey, who strode at Tam's side, peered into his face. Evening had fallen over the land, a beautiful gloaming that caressed the hills and gathered along the roadway, belying the turmoil in Tam's heart.

With the arrival of night, would Randleigh stay his lecherous advances on Annie? Tam feared not.

To old Archie, he said, "I intend to offer yon factor a bargain. He may no' accept, but it might serve to distract him and keep him occupied."

For one night—this night. And Tam could only hope a miracle accompanied the morning.

Archie shot him a curious look. "What will you offer?"

"Myself." The only thing he had, and a poor enough substitute for Annie. But God—or the powers, as Annie called them—knew it had all his love behind it. And love had to count for something.

He'd begun to believe love was the only thing that did count.

And in that case, he and Annie had made a great and wonderful difference in each other's lives. Never had he guessed when he watched her climb the steps of the platform back at the hiring fair what she would come to mean to him, or that he would one day be willing to sacrifice his own life for her sake.

225

But aye, perhaps his heart, far wiser than he, had always known.

"Aye," said Archie almost as if he heard Tam's thoughts, "you love your wife. And I ken fine what it is to love a woman. I would ha' traded my own life willingly to spare my Ciara the pain she endured before she passed. Your wee wife was able to bring her the only ease she knew. What cared I if 'twas gained through draughts or a wee spell or two? You ken, in the old days magic lived all over this land. 'Twas in the water; it breathed o'er the hills. And those who wrought it were nay slain but held above them all. What ha' we come to, lad, in our ignorance?"

"Perhaps," Tam proposed, surprising even himself with the observation, "'tis because we ha' turned our backs on the magic of our land these terrible things befall us. The land shrugs us off—wi' the factors' help."

"Perhaps so. But the land, lad—the land will always tak' us back again. 'Tis we maun shrug off the likes o' the factor."

****

"Wee Crow."

Surely, Annie thought, she had fallen asleep or swooned, in her extremity—surely she dreamed. Her uncle Dennis could not be sitting beside her in the tiny room, looking just as he had before his death. He could not be speaking to her, either, but the crow transformed into what could only be an image of him.

"Uncle Dennis? How is it you come here?"

"You called for help; when you call, Wee Crow, the natural world can only answer."

"You—you are dead."

"Tell me your mother taught you better than that! There is no death, not so long as the light endures. There is only transformation. I am in the breeze, in the flame, in the wave—and in the crow."

He smiled, and a strong current of reassurance flowed through Annie. But she said, "If you ha' come to help, then tell me what I may do. Randleigh will be here soon to demand his price for my life."

Dennis nodded. "He will. Shameful man, his greed rides him and gathers darkness within. Soon he will be able to see no light."

"How am I to turn him away this night? He is stronger than me—"

Dennis smiled again. "No one is stronger than you."

"He will threaten all I hold dear…Sonsie, Jockie, my precious beasts—Tam."

"Ah, Tam. Do you not wonder why he came to you? Like all the others, he came for healing—nay, not just to his hand. He came so he could rediscover his valiance in love. That, my dear Wee Crow, he is about to do. He finds it by putting you before himself. And is that not a wondrous gift to give?"

"Aye."

"Would you not be willing to sacrifice yourself in order to offer him that opportunity?"

Annie thought about it and frowned. "I would. But I would far rather we might be allowed to live peacefully in that love. I do no' see a way."

"Wee Crow, where is your faith?"

Annie laid her clasped hands against her breast. "It is here, inside. Uncle, I could defeat Randleigh if I reached for that power I ha' never yet used. I can feel it just waiting for me."

"It is always there," Dennis admitted.

"Why should I no' then grasp hold of it to protect those I love?"

"If you do, you will lose part of yourself."

"So shall I do if I let Randleigh use me this night. And did you no' just speak of sacrifice?"

"Lass, there is a man even now on his way here who brings you that gift of which we speak, his heart wrapped in brilliant courage. I ask again, will you steal from him the chance to make you that gift?"

Annie thought on it. "Nay, Uncle. But it terrifies me to think of him risking himself for my sake."

"Ah, and you would rather risk losing part of your soul, for his?"

The lock on the door rattled; the wraith that was Annie's uncle transformed back into a crow that flapped up to the window. The door opened, and Randleigh stepped in even as Annie struggled to her feet.

One look into the factor's face told her she would no longer be able to put him off. He had come for what he'd desired from the start, and she with but one weapon.

Dared she use it when everyone she loved bade her not? Should she submit to the dark lust she saw brimming in Randleigh's eyes? Would that buy her time? Should she instead seek to gather the light and make a shield that might endure a while, until Randleigh's cruelty broke her down?

"It is time, mistress. I will wait no longer."

He shut the door behind him and carefully locked it before dropping the key into his breast pocket. The room had become very nearly dark, only a trickle of dying daylight coming from the window where the crow still sat. Or did it? Was Annie alone?

She began to gather her forces—sadly depleted by fear and grief—and form a wall of protection around herself. At the very least she did not want to experience this horror, feel Randleigh inside her where only her Tam had been, suffer the same abuse he had dealt poor Kirstie.

She lifted her hand to him palm outward, and he stopped his advance.

"Ah, so you would employ your filthy magic against me, would you? But I shall tame the witch this night. By morn you will be crawling to me. Consider this: only your acceptance of me stays the slaughter of those beasts you value. Fight me or seek to harm me with your magic, and I will dispatch my men at once to your farm."

Annie threw back her head. "And if I should strangle you where you stand, so you canno' call to them? If I should stop the breath in your throat?"

"Then you will surely burn as a witch—not a magistrate in this land but will serve the sentence."

Annie looked into his eyes and believed him.

He smiled. "Take off your clothing, woman. I have waited long enough to see all of you."

Light tingling in her fingers, Annie bowed her head. *Help me*, she prayed again.

With a sudden flutter, the crow flew down from the window, a swooping shadow that dove for Randleigh's head. The wild flapping of its wings seemed to fill the tiny room, and Annie, ducking instinctively, raised her arms to shield her face. But the crow had a single target: cawing deafeningly, it pounced on Randleigh and tore at him with its talons, striking him again and again until he fell to the floor, cursing and scrabbling for the key in his pocket.

"Witch!" he cried as he at last succeeded in working the lock and crawling through the door. "You shall pay—you and your fiendish familiar."

The door slammed even as Annie started toward it; she heard the lock turn. The crow, having held the darkness at bay, flew back up to the window and away into the night.

Chapter Thirty-Four

Dawn broke just as Tam and Archie MacFey reached the laird's house, the pale light seeping across the sky and striking the gray stone. The place, all shut tight, had a bleak look, and alarm traveled through Tam even as he knocked at the door.

He could sense danger here, discord and darkness. He exchanged glances with MacFey, who shrugged uncomfortably, as if he too felt it.

Tam had to pound long at the door before anyone came. At last a manservant pulled it open and peered out at them.

"What is it?"

"I wish to see the factor."

"He is indisposed."

The apprehension in Tam's heart increased. What, just, did that mean? Did Randleigh linger even now with his Annie?

Outrage made him plant his good hand on the flat of the door and force it open. "I will see him, understand? I do no' care what he is about."

The young servant—perhaps a footman—backed up uncertainly. Tam and Archie stepped in.

"Wait here." The servant hurried off, leaving them standing in the chilly gloom of the entry, where Tam promptly stretched his inner senses. Annie was here—he could almost feel her—but where? In the strong room where he, Tam, had been held? And was she alone?

He discovered somewhat to his surprise that all his shame and fear had flown; shame at having failed to defend his parents and fear he would fail Annie now. He could not fail. He might have arrived too late to save her from Randleigh's vile touch, but he would free her somehow. Because nothing could stand against the sheer power of his love for her.

He knew that now. Annie had so taught him, the one true power was love.

The footman reappeared and told them, "This way."

Ned Randleigh occupied the parlor where they had been before; seated behind the big table where the magistrate, Belfour, had sat, he surged to his feet when Tam and Archie came in.

A man transfigured, however—he looked like he'd battled with someone wielding a sharp knife. Long gouges raked both cheeks and scored his forehead, trailed up into his brown hair. Several furrows intersected his eyes, so fresh they had not yet closed, and blood trickled out like pus.

"What has happened to you?" Tam wondered aloud.

"That is none of your affair." Randleigh's voice grated in his throat.

"Where is my wife?"

Randleigh's face twisted still further, and his lips worked before he spoke. "That vixen—the witch! She did this to me."

"She?" Tam stared, incredulous.

"Her familiar. She must have summoned it. I will

send my men to her house and destroy every one of her damned familiars."

Archie gasped, and Tam stepped up to the table. He glared across it at Randleigh, letting his anger show.

"Listen to me, factor: you have got what you deserve, all the evil you ha' done coming back upon you. Annie had nought to do wi' it. I am here to tell you: release her!"

"Oh, are you?" Randleigh drew back.

Tam's gaze ranged over the factor's wounds. "Would you truly risk further antagonizing those who protect her? Let her go."

"I will not. I cannot!"

"You must, or suffer still more."

Randleigh clenched his fists on top of the table. He slanted an ugly look at Archie MacFey. "Why are you here, old man?"

"I come to speak for Mistress Annie, to declare she is no' what you claim. There are others who will also come and speak to the magistrate and the priest of her goodness. Would you truly appear the fool before them all?"

"I cannot release her," Randleigh repeated, and gestured to himself. "Not now. I must save face."

A mad laugh threatened to bubble up in Tam's throat. Too late for that.

He leaned toward the factor. "You do no' wish to deal further with my wife. I tell you what you will do, if you wish to save face, and do it now before anyone else arrives. Release her and arrest me in her place. Say she has been found innocent but you ha' discovered the true culprit, the true threat, the influence attempting to turn her mind—me."

Randleigh stared at Tam in consternation. "Folk will never believe that."

"They will. They know little about me and ha' no ties to me, so will no' seek to protect me. You may do your worst: flog me, torture me to win a confession, put out my eyes, burn me—I do no' care so long as you henceforth leave her in peace."

Archie MacFey gasped again, and Randleigh reared back like a balky horse. "You would give yourself up for that wanton vixen?"

"Willingly. But she is neither wanton nor a vixen. She is my wife. Tell everyone I misled her, and vent your spleen on this flesh." Tam did laugh then. "Save your face."

"Master Sutherland." Archie laid his hand on Tam's arm. "You canno'—"

"Do you no' see, Archie, he has no power over me?" Not so long as Tam had Annie's love. He had but one desire: to spend himself now in return for that love.

He waved his injured hand. "Make a spectacle of it, if you wish, your bold statement against witchcraft. Invite all the tenants, let them see me suffer. But you will release her now, this moment, and vow ne'er to harm her again. That is the bargain on the table—the only bargain."

"You are mad," Randleigh breathed.

"I am not. Give me your agreement, Ned Randleigh. But remember you one thing—every evil act, all the hurt and harm you put out into the world, will return upon you *times three*."

"You curse me!" Wildly, Randleigh turned to Archie MacFey. "You hear him."

"He does hear me, factor. You'd better arrest me

for it."

Randleigh stared into Tam's eyes and encountered complete conviction.

"Guards!" he bellowed frantically. "Here to me!"

****

"You are free to go."

Ned Randleigh did not look Annie in the eyes as he swung wide the door of her prison. She gaped at him in shock and emitted but one strangled sound. "Eh?"

"Leave. Your presence is no longer required."

Annie stared at the factor's half-averted face while her heart rose on a surge of hope, only to fall again sickeningly. Streaked with blood and gouges inflicted by the crow's beak and talons, his countenance betrayed little. Yet he must be toying with Annie, letting her think she might get away before slamming the door on her again.

She drew an aching breath. "How is this? Why are you releasing me?"

"The true culprit has been seized."

"Culprit? What is that you say?" After all the hours of confinement, Annie's wits did not move swiftly enough. Had Randleigh perhaps captured the crow?

Randleigh did look at her then, a stare of hate so sharp it stabbed her.

"He has bought your freedom. Would you rather stay and die with him?"

"He? Who?"

"Go home. And I would suggest you pack up your mangy animals and your halfwit servants and leave the district while you can."

Trembling from head to foot, Annie stepped out of the strong room. With Randleigh a mute presence at her back, she went through the silent, gloomy house to the front door, seeing no one on the way. Only steps from freedom, she paused.

"Tell me who—"

Randleigh reached past her, which brought him far too close, and hauled open the door.

"I know now why the two of you are together and why you prefer him to me. I shall exorcise the evil in him—and perhaps in so doing chase it from you also."

"Who?" Annie demanded again, but her heart knew—impossible, terrifying! For Randleigh could accuse her of preferring only one man.

"Nay. Nay, tell me 'tis no' true." She actually reached for the detested Randleigh as if she might shake the words from him.

"Your dark master."

"Do you speak of my husband? You have arrested Tam?"

"Ah, so you name him. Another admission for the priest when he arrives."

"The priest? You mean to put Tam Sutherland on trial for witchcraft?" Annie's knees did fail her then. She sank to the floor, but Randleigh, seizing her arm, dragged her up again and thrust her through the open doorway. Beyond, she saw one of her neighbors, Archie MacFey, waiting.

"Nay," she begged Randleigh frantically. "Take me instead. I will do aught you ask—go to your bed, give you all of what you ha' wanted from me. Only let Tam Sutherland go."

"Harlot witch," Randleigh sneered, and slammed the door in her face.

Chapter Thirty-Five

"My fault, it is all my fault."

Sitting at her own table, before her a steaming mug of broth she dared not touch, Annic could do nothing but lament. Sonsie had forced the broth on her, but she knew if she took so much as a sip she would lose it again just as quickly.

Sonsie now bustled around the room, spending her agitation by doing senseless chores while Annie's animals clustered near her—Ruff pressed close to her side, wee Ella in her lap, even Mairi the fox huddled at her feet. Sol had not taken his yellow eyes from her since her return. Her relief at seeing them all not withstanding, Annie took small comfort.

Archie MacFey still remained on the farm, now outside helping care for Old Rake, who had been led back into the byre. Archie had walked her home and explained to her what Tam Sutherland had done.

Sacrificed himself for her. Traded his life for hers, purchased her future and taken on all the pain Randleigh meant to inflict—Randleigh's cruelty, masquerading as justice. She'd comprehended that the moment the words *your dark master* fell from Ned Randleigh's lips. And in that instant she'd felt Tam's love wrap around her like a living shield, woven by his valiant heart.

Had ever a man loved as Tam Sutherland loved?

Had ever courage burned so bright? She sat, while the animals cuddled around her and Sonsie chattered nervously, and remembered it all.

The first glimpse she'd caught of him at the hiring fair, the instant spear of attraction that passed through her when their gazes met. The surge of wild hope in her heart when she wondered if she might have him for husband, before she saw his hand and forced herself to dismiss him as too poor a candidate in Ned Randleigh's eyes.

Dismiss it as she would, fate had brought her and Tam together, or perhaps something far more vital and immediate than fate—the light by which Annie lived.

She remembered the first time she had touched him, the first time their lips had met. And the night, in her bed, he had claimed her for his own, trading a part of himself to her even as she gave herself to him without reservation.

How could the darkness—even that Ned Randleigh harbored—defeat so much light?

Yet she knew that good and fine people had been falsely accused and slain before now. Could she honor this choice Tam made and accept the grand gift he presented her, resign herself to never touching him again or gazing into his eyes, inhaling his warm scent? She could be certain of only one thing.

The darkness might rear up against the light. It could never defeat the love.

Her love for Tam Sutherland, she knew, would endure forever, as would this selfless act of his. If he went to his grave, her heart went with him. And if she lived she might breathe air, work with her hands in service to others, and do her best to carry on; she would never love any man but Tam Sutherland.

****

"I maun be there."

Annie had come to that conclusion sometime during the endless night when she contemplated ways she could—and could not—assist Tam. She'd once again considered fighting darkness with darkness, but her heart knew Tam had made his sacrifice to keep her from that path. What should she give him save her support?

Her friends and neighbors seemed to agree. They had started arriving just after dawn and now gathered in her house and yard, their attitudes much changed from what they'd been at the market.

Some of that might be due to the tale Archie MacFey had told over and over again, declaring Tam's courage and his belief in his wife's goodness.

Or perhaps the night had dealt with people's hearts as it had Annie's; mayhap they too had begun remembering the light her mother had shed like kindness, a tradition Annie had striven hard to continue.

But she must be her own woman now, follow her own heart.

"Mistress," Kirstie said earnestly, "I do no' think it a good idea for you to go and witness what will happen at the laird's house."

"Aye," several men agreed.

They had, many of them, brought word of what Randleigh planned for this day: a public questioning of Tam Sutherland, heard by magistrate and priest, the finding of a sentence, and public execution either by axe or flame.

"Aye," Archie echoed his neighbors. "That young

man has a valiant heart—to that I can attest. But he will no' want you to witness his suffering."

Suffering. As if Tam Sutherland had not already suffered enough on her account. What would it be now? Hot irons? Knives?

Annie looked around the room wildly at her friends, neighbors, and beloved animals. Sol had flown out the window just before daylight and not returned, no doubt sensing the incipient arrival of so many. But the rest of the animals stood by her, wee Ella—so bonded with Tam—whimpering.

She lifted her chin. "I will be there and pay tribute to this great sacrifice he makes for my sake. I would appreciate any of you willing to come with me."

Perhaps a miracle would still occur, and they could prevent this travesty.

But aye, it would require a miracle.

In the end, Rory MacBain took her in his cart, everyone else, including Ruff, trailing along. They moved down the roads to the laird's house under a lowering sky, and the sun drifted higher and higher in the east, shedding red like a gout of blood.

A terrible bad omen that, as Annie knew, but she spoke a prayer as she rode, fervently suing protection not for herself but for the man she loved.

For as she knew, one man's bad omen could prove good to another at odds with him. So might it be.

Chapter Thirty-Six

"This is the accused, one Tam Sutherland," Randleigh announced as Tam was led into the room. The laird's parlor, which the factor seemed to have adopted for his own, was now occupied by several men.

Tam blinked at them. After the near-dark of the strong room, even the gloomy parlor seemed too bright. He'd spent the night—his last in this world?—with thoughts of Annie, garnering strength for what must come, and could fair feel her with him, her love a living presence.

It gave him courage even now, when he saw what awaited him.

A priest, though not Father Alban, and another man who could only be the afore-absent magistrate, not Mr. Belfour with whom Tam had found favor last time.

Aye, and what had he expected? Randleigh could not afford to lose this time. He must—in his own words—save face before all the folk he lived to subjugate. Such men as he thrived on the fear and respect of others.

Tam would show him neither.

He eyed the two men meant to pass sentence upon him, and they scrutinized him in turn. The priest had a pale face and thin hair that barely covered an arched dome. His eyes moved nervously, and Tam wondered of what he might be afraid. God? Damnation? Ned

Randleigh?

The magistrate, by contrast, looked florid and overfed. Surely it must be too early for him to have started drinking, yet his eyes appeared bleary and bored.

No hope of justice here, then—nor mercy.

Had Tam truly hoped for any?

"He does not look much like a great warlock," the magistrate observed.

"Often they do not," contributed the priest. "That is how they trick and seduce others. If he is what you claim, Master Randleigh, he will have the Devil's mark upon him." His pale tongue poked out and wetted his lips. "Have him take off his clothes."

The magistrate gave the priest a sideways stare, but Randleigh only said, "Not here, Father—outside. A crowd gathers even now. Let them see that I carry this out properly, let them witness the triumph of righteousness."

A crowd? For the first time, Tam's hard-won courage wavered. Not Annie, let it not include Annie! He could not bear for her to witness his pain.

The priest took a step nearer. "You say he cursed you?"

"So he did, Father. Wished all manner of evil down upon me."

"Is this true, man?" The magistrate addressed Tam directly. "Do you so confess to being a practitioner of the dark arts and a servant of Lucifer?"

"I do not." To Tam's own surprise his voice sounded steady. He summoned up a picture of Annie's face in his mind: her smile, the passion in her eyes when he came to her.

If he protected her now, his life would be well spent.

"Aye, so," said the priest. "Let us begin. He shall scream his confession before 'tis done."

****

The crowd in front of the laird's house had grown restless. They milled about, eyed the stone façade of the mansion, and muttered to one another.

Annie, trying not to succumb to the sickness that gripped her, felt strung tight enough to break. She could sense so many things: the emotions of those around her, including Kirstie, Jockie, Archie, and her other supporters; the darkness that virtually breathed from inside the house.

The beat of Tam's heart, still linked with hers.

What would she feel if that heart stopped beating? Would hers cease also in sympathy?

She bent her head and whispered a prayer, suing the powers of the air, fire, water, and earth for protection—not of her but of Tam. As she now saw all too well, it was one and the same.

No sooner had she raised her circle than the door opened. A man in a black frock coat stepped out first— a priest, but not Father Alban. Next came two guards, pistols at their sides, and then…

Annie's heart leaped with hopeless, helpless love and pride. For Tam Sutherland came with his head high, his gaze steady even though they had bound his hands behind him—och, pity his poor, broken fingers! But they would do far worse to him this day, before it ended.

She blinked back a rush of tears; she would not let Tam see her terror. For he moved with the same natural dignity that had marked him at the hiring fair. And she refused to insult such courage with weakness.

She willed him to look for her, to see her, and his gaze swept through the onlookers until it located her. Emotion shone clear then in his eyes—consternation? Gladness? Perhaps both tangled together.

My love, she thought, and his head lifted higher still.

My love.

Behind him, nearly overlooked by Annie, came Ned Randleigh and another man, who had a round, flushed face.

Randleigh stepped to the top of the stone steps which edged a wide porch—wide enough for this vile pantomime he played—and spoke.

"It is well you have all come. No doubt many of you know that a viper has been nesting in our midst, stealing good will and working evil. This individual feigned a fair and helpful demeanor all while plotting against us."

Randleigh's eyes, just like Tam's, swept the crowd until they found Annie; he focused on her with satisfaction.

Aye, and he would pay her back for spurning him by harming that for which she cared most in the world.

Randleigh raised his voice still higher in a victorious howl. "Witches still exist among us! I am here to tell you so; the great witch trials of the past did not serve to eradicate them all. Only ask your priest!" He swept the black-clad man forward with a wave of his arm but did not let him speak. "Righteousness will serve to obliterate the darkness."

If only it would, Annie thought, stifling a sob. If

only it would.

"This man"—Randleigh pointed at Tam—"is a powerful warlock. Since his arrival here, he has been busy poisoning the district, and he has admitted his guilt—"

"That I deny!" Tam threw back his head and shouted.

Randleigh spun to face him; the two men glared at one another in a contest of wills Annie felt where she stood.

"He will be brought to admit it here before you all," Randleigh amended. "Our magistrate will pass sentence upon him, and the good father, here, will carry it out. Justice will be done this day."

Tam Sutherland would die. Because for all his bright courage he stood in Ned Randleigh's power, and Randleigh would see this thing done.

Annie wanted to fly forward, to rail against Randleigh—to sacrifice herself even as Tam had done for her. The look on Tam's face stopped her, held her, reminded her that this great act, his gift to her, came of his love. But och, she could not bear to stand and watch.

She squeezed her eyes shut and again began to pray, prayed as she had never done before.

"Seize him!" Randleigh's hated voice interrupted her prayer, and the crowd stirred and muttered. "Strip him down. Bring the irons."

Nay—nay, not that. Annie had heard tales of men and women writhing as the heated metal met their flesh, and in the end confessing to anything—*anything*—just to make the agony stop.

Please, she prayed.

A loud rattling came from well behind her as a cart turned in off the road and entered the yard. The crowd parted to make way for it as grass parts before a strong wind, but it could not come far for all the bodies in the way. Eventually the driver drew the horse to a halt and the passenger beside him got to his feet, surveying the scene.

Father Alban.

Annie's heart leaped on another surge of hope. Could the priest do something to stop this madness?

"Father!" Annie cried, and the priest found her with his gaze. He then looked to the steps where he considered Randleigh, Tam, and his fellow clergyman in turn.

"In the name of God, what goes on here?"

"We are trying a witch," answered the other priest. "And no concern, Father, of yours."

"If that does not concern me," Father Alban announced, descending from the cart, "I do not know what does."

Chapter Thirty-Seven

The breath Tam had been holding left him in a rush when he saw Father Alban, and for the first time hope stirred in his heart.

Though Tam doubted the priest had approved of his marriage to Annie, the man now looked angrier than a hive of bees and full of righteous intent. He issued from the cart and swept to the foot of the steps as people moved aside respectfully.

The other priest stepped out and met him at the edge of the porch. "You are not needed here," he told Father Alban. "This is not your patch or your parish."

"If it is yours, brother, you should be ashamed of yourself. A witch trial? Are we not more enlightened than that?"

"Evil is evil and must be scotched wherever it is found."

"This man is not evil." Father Alban pointed dramatically at Tam. "Nor is his wife. I have known her from a wee lass—"

Randleigh stepped forward. "You do not know everything, Father. He has admitted his sin to me privately and will now do so before all."

Father Alban looked Tam in the eye. "What say you to this, Tam Sutherland?"

Tam lifted his chin higher. "That my wife is a good and innocent woman. If anyone shall be prosecuted for witchcraft here today, it will be me."

"That is what I thought," said Father Alban. He turned on Randleigh with still more heat. "I know what you are about, man. Even in Oban we have heard the stories. You cannot protect yourself by seeking to harm others."

"You know nothing, priest, as to what my responsibilities are. Laird Ardaugh left me here in his stead with all his authority. I shall so act. Now step back out of the way, unless you wish for my men to restrain you as well."

The people in the crowd shifted uneasily, and Father Alban bristled. "You would not dare—"

Randleigh nodded at his men who guarded the steps. "Seize him."

The onlookers gasped. Several men started forward, which carried Annie nearer Tam. She gazed into his face, yearning.

"I will stand here," Father Alban halted them all, "and observe. I will report to the bishop all that transpires here today. God's will be done!"

As if on cue, the skies opened and a cold rain streaked down, making those gathered exclaim again. In mere moments, everyone in the yard became soaked to the skin.

Just as if the very elements lamented this travesty, Tam thought.

He steeled himself as Randleigh's men took hold of him and the factor turned to focus that gaze, colder than the rain, on his face.

"Set the brazier beneath the overhang and prepare him. His dark arts will not delay our work here."

Randleigh's men grappled with Tam and tore the

shirt from him, disregarding his bound hands. The crowd shifted forward as one. A strangled sound came from Annie's throat.

Tam dared not look at her now. If he did, he feared his longing would get the better of him and undermine his hard-won resolution.

Only give me the strength I will need, he prayed.

Several things happened then in quick succession. A large, furry form hurtled up the stone steps, streaked past Randleigh, and threw itself at the man on Tam's left.

"Kill that beast!" Randleigh cried. "'Tis the warlock's familiar!"

"Nay!" Annie wailed and darted forward to follow Ruff up the steps. The big dog heeded neither Randleigh nor the man trying to fend him off; his growls rose to fill the air.

And agony filled Annie's eyes. Near enough now for him to touch, Tam did not know if she feared more for him or the valiant dog.

"Witch!" Randleigh bellowed and pointed his finger at her. "The warlock has surely sought to contaminate this woman."

Tam lost all the breath in his body. He wanted to leap forward, defend Annie, but Randleigh's henchmen held him still, one with a heated iron in his hand.

He waved it dangerously at Ruff, and Annie threw herself on the animal in an effort to protect him.

Randleigh strode forward, wrested the iron from his man, and declared, "Let justice be done!"

He brought the glowing iron down in a swoop aimed at Tam's naked chest, and Tam steeled himself for the ensuing pain.

It never came.

Instead, even as Annie cried out, both her arms wrapped around Ruff, a great brown bird descended from the lowering sky, seeming to materialize out of the pelting rain, and flew at Ned Randleigh's head, flapping wildly.

Randleigh gave a hoarse cry and raised both arms to protect his head. The heated iron fell from his hand and clattered harmlessly onto the stones even as Tam's captors shied, pulling him away. The crowd gasped as one, either at the spectacle of seeing an owl fly in daylight or the persistence with which Sol attacked the factor, using wings, beak, and talons.

Randleigh went down beneath the onslaught, new blood appearing where the previous furrows had barely closed.

In the furor, no one—including Tam—heard a carriage pull into the forecourt. Yet a ripple of movement began as the crowd shifted aside for someone, and a commanding voice made itself heard above Randleigh's cries.

"What goes on here? Someone tell me what is happening. Mistress Ann!"

Annie, still clutching Ruff tightly, spun as did everyone else present save Ned Randleigh, who remained kneeling on the stone, even after Sol rose into the air and flapped away in near silence.

"Laird Ardaugh," she breathed.

The sour-faced priest and the florid magistrate both stiffened, and Tam's captors let go of him. He followed Annie's gaze, and his eyes narrowed.

Aye, and so this must be the absentee laird returned at last from Edinburgh. Looking at him, Tam found it possible to believe he had been ill all this while, unable to respond to Annie's pleas. For even now he did not come under his own power. White-haired, pale, and slow-moving, he leaned on the arm of a burly ghillie who half carried him up the steps, where he paused, staring at the scene in disbelief.

Another man followed him. Tam recognized the physician, Master Camden, whom Annie had brought to tend his hand. All the breath left his body in a rush, even as Ned Randleigh lifted his head and scrambled to his feet.

Laird Ardaugh visibly recoiled upon seeing Randleigh's countenance streaked with rain and blood.

"What is the meaning of this?" the laird demanded of his factor.

"A witch trial, my laird," Randleigh replied hoarsely.

"What!" Ardaugh exchanged incredulous looks with his companions before gesturing to Tam. "Who is this man?"

"The—the witch."

"Seize him," Ardaugh said to the men at Tam's back, and his heart fell violently yet again. But the men stepped past him at Ardaugh's nod and caught hold of Ned Randleigh even as Ruff pressed against Tam's side.

Laird Ardaugh turned to survey the crowd of his tenants through the streaming rain. "Enough of this madness! I regret, my good folk, I have been away so long—long enough to allow such a travesty on our lands. I have neglected you, but I am returned. We shall get to the bottom of your complaints—that I do vow!"

A ragged cheer arose to compete with Randleigh's

cries as he was dragged away into the house.

Laird Ardaugh turned to Annie, whose face shone with light. "You, lass, come with me and tell me all I need to know."

"Aye, Laird. And please may I bring my husband?"

Ardaugh turned shrewd eyes on Tam where he stood swaying.

"Well, aye, and I think you should."

Chapter Thirty-Eight

Despite his physical weakness, Laird Ardaugh swept through the house like a strong wave, with Annie, Tam, and several others in his wake. Annie, clutching her husband's arm and pressed close to his side, tried to reconcile the laird's presence and failed. Terrible changed the man was—so much so that she barely recognized him.

They made for the parlor, where Laird Ardaugh immediately ordered a fire kindled.

"And brandy," he added to the servants who had flocked to him, "if there be any in the house."

He then eyed everyone before sinking into a chair, where Camden, the physician, bent over him in concern.

A dream, Annie told herself—such it must be, one conjured from the pieces of the impossible horror outside.

Yet Tam's arm, bare and wet, seemed real beneath her fingers. She could feel him trembling, could sense his mingled relief and disbelief that matched her own. Master Camden, here? And Ruff, dripping wet, in the Laird's parlor, apparently having followed them in? Father Alban, as well as the priest Randleigh had brought, and the florid magistrate?

Despite her grip on Tam's arm, she swayed where she stood.

Ardaugh fixed her with a shrewd gaze and waved a hand. "You'd better sit down, the two of you." He then turned his eyes on the florid man. "I want explanations. Who are you and why are you here?"

The man, who seemed to have lost some of his color and arrogance, said, "Sir, I am Major Rodney Eddlesfield, acting magistrate of this district."

Ardaugh lifted his frail hand. "Are you? Who appointed you such? And where is Alexander MacKenzie, who acted as magistrate in my time?"

"I believe Master MacKenzie is dead, my laird. Ned Randleigh appointed me."

"Did he! By what authority?"

"He said it was by your authority, Laird Ardaugh."

Ardaugh exchanged glances once more with the physician. "Just as you said, Doctor—the man has been using my name without my consent." He switched his gaze back to Eddlesfield. Frail as the rest of him might now be, that stare still held power. "It looks to me as if he paid you off in whisky and kept you in his pocket. Get out of my sight." Ardaugh waved an arm, and Eddlesfield, with a speaking look at the priest, took himself from the room.

"And you?" Ardaugh looked next at the priest. "Who are you?"

The priest, apparently frozen in his dismay, said nothing.

Ardaugh turned to Father Alban. "Do you know your fellow clergyman, Father?"

Father Alban shot a kindly look at Annie before he replied, "I know of him, my laird—many in the Highlands have heard about him, an itinerant priest bent on persecution and the elimination of what he calls evil."

Ardaugh huffed. "Such ugliness is a thing of the past. We have become enlightened, even here in the Highlands. Surely between us, Father Alban, you and I can see him defrocked?"

The sour-faced priest bristled. "I will continue to be vigilant in my pursuit of righteousness."

"Well, you will not do it here," Ardaugh declared. "Get him out of my sight as well."

Even as one of his coachmen showed the priest out, Ardaugh returned his gaze to Annie where she now sat on a small sofa, Tam pressed to her side and Ruff at her knee.

"As for you, Mistress MacCallum—or I gather it is Mistress Sutherland now..." One corner of his mouth tightened. "I received your letters. I owe you an apology; for a time I was too ill to read them or to see you when you journeyed to Edinburgh. I owed better to my old friend, your uncle—and to you."

Annie, not knowing what to say to that, nodded.

"My malady," the laird went on in a slightly stronger voice, "is one that besets many of my contemporaries all about the Highlands—poverty combined with age and shame. Shame, aye, lass—that I sold too many rights to my creditors in the south, along with my conscience. What would your good uncle say to that, eh? He would point out to me the extent of my duty, bid me stop licking my wounds, and think again of those who rely on me."

His gaze narrowed on Annie's face. "As you have done in his stead, through your letters. If one part of what you have related be true, lass, I should be horsewhipped for letting it occur. Well? What do you say for yourself?"

"Every word I wrote to you, my laird, was truth. You can speak to your folk if you wish to confirm it all. Ned Randleigh has been terrorizing this district, and most especially the women here."

"I shall certainly speak with any who will come to me. I owe them that. But I can see by what was in progress when I arrived how far things have slipped in my absence. Add to that the fact that Master Camden, here, came to see me personally, assessed my condition, and advised me of what was going on. I read your letters then, lass. I gathered my strength and made the journey home. I know it is late, but I trust it will count for something."

Annie looked at the physician. "Thank you, sir. Thank you so very much. You ha' saved my husband's life."

Camden smiled at her kindly. "A bit like you, Mistress Sutherland, I am bound to alleviate suffering wherever I find it."

Father Alban stepped forward and addressed Annie also. "Why did you not tell me all of what was going on here, lass, when I performed your marriage?"

Annie shook her head. "Ned Randleigh's power seemed so absolute, I did not think anyone but the man who'd appointed him could set him down. I should have known better; all of you went out of your way to help us, in the end."

She stopped speaking, struck by a sudden thought, for she saw now with blinding clarity: the law by which she lived her life held true. The light she had put out into the world had returned to her threefold.

Tam spoke, his voice harsh. "If I may ask, what

will happen to Ned Randleigh?"

Laird Ardaugh switched his gaze to Tam. "Ah, the husband. You, it appears, were willing to accept much of Randleigh's abuse in defense of your wife."

Tam replied simply, "I would do aught in the world to protect her."

"Master Camden, here, has told me what Randleigh did to your hand, and a bit of what befell you before that, in the north." Ardaugh grimaced. "'Twas a long and arduous ride from Edinburgh. It grieves me, young man, what trouble now besets the Highlands. The old way of life passes, and I am as guilty as any of failing to halt the changes. Alas, I have not the wealth left to compensate you as you deserve. But I can promise both you and Annie things here will improve. We may all live in poverty, and extreme poverty, at that. But we shall do so together."

Annie asked, "Does that mean you will stay, Laird Ardaugh?"

"It does. I will sell my house in Edinburgh and die here, where I was born." He drew a breath. "For I am an old man and without issue—save those who live here on this land with me. Best to stop feeling sorry for myself, eh, and begin thinking of them?"

Annie blinked away tears. "Laird Ardaugh, what will the future hold?"

"After I am dead, you mean? I do not know yet. But I can promise there will be no further clearances on my land."

Relief struck Annie so hard it made her dizzy; Tam's fingers tightened on hers almost painfully.

"Thank you," she breathed.

"Nay, lass, it is I who must thank you and your

husband for keeping the faith even when I failed you. Your mother and uncle would be proud of you. Now, where is that brandy? Your husband needs a tot, unless I miss my guess."

"Aye, my laird," Tam agreed, sounding dazed.

Ardaugh fixed an eye on him. "I know little enough of you, sir, save what I saw when I arrived, and that speaks well of your courage, along with the fact that Annie, here, chose you. I think we shall deal well together. As I say, I am an old man. I shall need a new factor, one who acts in wisdom and compassion. Might I hope you will consider taking that place?"

Annie watched as light—quiet yet powerful—filled her husband's eyes. With the dignity which had marked him from the first, he replied.

"My laird, I would be honored."

Chapter Thirty-Nine

"Are you certain you are fit for this?" Annie turned in the bed to face the man beside her and strove to read his expression in the dim light.

The house had at last gone quiet, everything back in its place. Sonsie slept up in the loft, Ella curled at Tam's feet, and Ruff lay at the side of the bed within reach of Annie's hand. The fox and the cats cuddled together by the fire, and Annie could just see Sol—who must have accomplished his flight to the laird's house and back again in stages—on his perch by the window, outlined against the slightly paler night sky.

The room might look the same, yet she knew everything had changed. For the better, she trusted. All for the better.

Yet she could not seem to help fussing over Tam. Her terror when she'd beheld him in Randleigh's power, knowing he meant to sacrifice himself for her, would not let go.

"More than fit," he murmured in reply, and his lips brushed her cheek. "Can you no' tell?"

She wanted him to love her, longed for a bonding wild and deep, desired it with intensity that half frightened her. Tam Sutherland lay in her heart now; he had become part of her soul.

But, she reflected, that might well have happened the first time she saw him at the hiring fair.

"I can tell. But"—she ran her fingers down his chest just for the pleasure of it—"I barely believe you are safe and here wi' me. When I think what that man meant to do to you, what you would ha' endured for my sake…"

He drew her close against him, a ship coming in to harbor. "I would do anything for you, Annie Sutherland. Anything. Do you no' ken how I love you?"

"I do." She could scarcely doubt, with the proof of it just behind them. "And I hope you know how I love you."

"I think I can tell." He gathered her still closer, using his good hand. A measure of the terrible fear inside Annie eased then, subsiding into a glorious contentment.

"And," he whispered, "I hope you are proud of what you've done this day."

"Me, proud?" She studied his face in the dim light, knowing she would never tire of its lean lines or of his understated humor, and that she could never, never get enough of this man. "'Tis yoursel' was the hero."

"Ah, nay—if there is a hero, 'tis the good physician, Master Camden, who traveled all the way to Edinburgh and used his influence to see the laird—and treat him, I do no' doubt, so he might travel back here."

"There is but one hero of my heart."

She pressed her lips to his in a lingering kiss, which he received with satisfaction before he spoke again.

"But, Wee Crow, 'tis you brought about the miracle that transpired this day, with your believing. Do you no see? The light you ha' been shining out into the world returned to you full well through those like Jockie and Kirstie who stood wi' you, the valiance o' your animals, and all those who took our part."

"I do see that, aye. All conspired together to bring about the downfall of that evil, wretched man—"

"Ah, now." Tam stayed her words by laying gentle fingers across her lips. "Do no' speak such hate."

"But…"

"I ha' learned, and learned the hard way, hatred is a poison that galls the one who hates. Look what it did to me—nearly did to me, but for the love of you. Nay, Annie, you have taught me to put faith only in light, if I will ha' it back in turn."

Annie's eyes filled with tears. "I am glad."

"Anyway…" He drew a breath, and a new note entered his voice. "I am thinking we should be grateful to Ned Randleigh."

"Grateful?" She thrashed in his arms. "To the man who nearly destroyed us? Och, Tam, now you go too far."

"But he did no' destroy us." Tam kissed her. "He could no'." Another soft kiss that turned Annie weak inside. "And were it no' for Randleigh and his black heart, you would no' ha' come to the hiring fair, would you?"

"Most likely not."

"And so never would ha' made your braw announcement asking for a husband."

"Ah, this is true."

"And never would ha' looked twice at me."

"I would!"

"Ne'er ha' wed me," Tam amended, landing yet another kiss on her lips.

"Well, so."

"And I would no' be here with you, able to love you this whole night long."

Annie sighed, leaving go of her worry and hurt. "There is that," she murmured in pure bliss. "Blessed be the hiring fair."

A word about the author…

Born and raised in Western New York, Laura Strickland has pursued lifelong interests in lore, legend, magic, and music, all reflected in her writing. Though her imagination frequently takes her to far-off places, she is usually happiest at home not far from Lake Ontario with her husband and her "fur" child, a rescue dog.

Author of Scottish romances as well as the Guardians of Sherwood trilogy, she has also published three Buffalo Steampunk romances, two Christmas novellas, a Valentine's Day short story, and two Lobster Cove historical romances so far, all available from The Wild Rose Press, Inc. (See a list of her titles in the first pages of this book.)

Thank you for purchasing
this publication of The Wild Rose Press, Inc.

If you enjoyed the story, we would appreciate your
letting others know by leaving a review.

For other wonderful stories,
please visit our on-line bookstore at
www.thewildrosepress.com.

For questions or more information
contact us at
info@thewildrosepress.com.

The Wild Rose Press, Inc.
www.thewildrosepress.com

Stay current with The Wild Rose Press, Inc.

Like us on Facebook

https://www.facebook.com/TheWildRosePress

And Follow us on Twitter
https://twitter.com/WildRosePress

www.ingramcontent.com/pod-product-compliance
Lightning Source LLC
Chambersburg PA
CBHW070328260626
47160CB00003B/979